"How long are you staying?" Chloe asked Evan.

Evan raised their joined hands to brush his lips across her knuckles. "My return flight isn't until the end of the week."

Heat rose between them as they danced, and her gaze locked with his. For two cents he'd drag her out and say to hell with the husband.

"I'm married," she whispered, regret filming her eyes. "Daniel's a good man. I can't betray him."

Evan felt a sharp stab of pain over what he'd lost. He almost felt as if he'd been betrayed. He'd been careless with women's feelings before, but no one had ever mattered to him the way Chloe did. Until this moment he hadn't even realized how strong his feelings were. "Daniel might be your lawful husband," he said, "but you'll always belong to me. Before I go may I kiss the bride?"

She nodded and he lowered his mouth to hers in a brief kiss that was achingly sweet and salted by tears. Evan cradled Chloe in his arms, lost in emotion and not knowing how he'd gotten that way.

A large hand grasped his arm, pulling Evan back. Damn, it was Daniel. Evan cast a last glance at Chloe and then released her. "She's all yours, mate," he said roughly to Daniel. "For now."

Dear Reader,

What makes for a lasting marriage? I believe certain things are important—common goals, shared history, respect, understanding and the ability to forgive. And perhaps most important, the deeply held belief that love is true, that it's worth fighting for, sacrificing for and having faith in when all seems lost.

I thoroughly enjoyed writing this story about a love that spans decades. I've been married to the same wonderful man for over twenty years. I've experienced the ups and downs that come with any long-term relationship. When love is true, all the hardships and struggles are rewarded by the richness and joy that come from loving a lifelong partner.

I hope you enjoy Daniel and Chloe's story. I love to hear from readers. You can e-mail me at www.joankilby.com or write to me at P.O. Box 234, Point Roberts, WA 98281-0234.

Sincerely,

Joan

When Love Is True

Joan Kilby

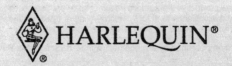

HARLEQUIN®

TORONTO • NEW YORK • LONDON
AMSTERDAM • PARIS • SYDNEY • HAMBURG
STOCKHOLM • ATHENS • TOKYO • MILAN • MADRID
PRAGUE • WARSAW • BUDAPEST • AUCKLAND

ISBN-13: 978-0-373-65412-3
ISBN-10:   0-373-65412-X

WHEN LOVE IS TRUE

ABOUT THE AUTHOR

When Joan Kilby isn't working on her next romance novel she can often be found sipping a latte at a sidewalk café and indulging in her favorite pastime of people watching. Originally from Vancouver, Canada, Joan now lives in Australia with her husband and three children. She enjoys cooking as a creative outlet and gets some of her best ideas while watching her Jack Russell terrier chase waves at the beach.

Books by Joan Kilby

HARLEQUIN SUPERROMANCE

★The Wilde Men

To Mike

Chapter 1

*T*wo sets of bubbles rose from the scuba divers off the west coast of Vancouver Island. Chloe Bennett, wrapped in a duffel coat against the chill January air, watched the spreading ripples intersect and wondered which set of bubbles belonged to her husband, Daniel, and which belonged to Evan, her former lover?

Her nineteen-year-old daughter, Brianna, poked about in tide pools, and Chloe could see her glowing blond head as she wandered between granite boulders as large and smooth as a whale's back. Other questions surfaced, which Chloe had given up pondering years earlier. Who had fathered the child who'd brought her and Daniel to the altar—Evan or her husband?

Chloe worried about Daniel. Evan was a highly experi-

enced scuba diver, but Daniel was a novice and this deep-water shipwreck was quite possibly beyond his present capability. Only Chloe knew that his confidence was at least partly feigned. Only she knew he was there in large part because he was determined not to show weakness in front of his rival.

She wrapped her duffel coat tighter and shivered at the memory of the rage in Daniel's eyes as the men had suited up on the cobblestone beach between the towering cedar trees. She understood his hostility toward Evan, but why had he turned on her? Was it possible Daniel had overheard her conversation with Evan at the house before the dive?

Twenty years earlier…

"Don't cry, sweetheart." Esme dabbed at the delicate skin beneath her daughter's eyes and the damp tissue came away smudged with dark brown mascara. "This is the happiest day of your life."

"I think I'm going to be sick." Chloe swallowed and pressed a trembling hand to her stomach, which was cinched tight in ivory satin. A worn pair of ballet shoes hung by their pink ribbons from a knob on her old brass bed, a reminder of the career she was giving up just as she was reaching her peak.

"Nerves," Esme pronounced with a bright smile. "All brides get cold feet before the ceremony." She tossed away the used tissue and pushed at Chloe's wispy red-gold bangs with her beringed fingers. "Turn around and let me adjust your veil."

"Mom, stop!" Chloe clutched her mother's wrists with icy fingers. "It's not nerves. It's morning sickness."

Esme's dark blue eyes widened. "You're joking."

"I wish I was," Chloe said bitterly. "Why do you think I'm getting married?"

"I'd hoped it was for love." Esme's gaze skimmed Chloe's thin, muscular figure for any hint of a pregnancy. "You've only been seeing Daniel for a few months. Before that you were head over heels for that Australian doctor who went to work in the refugee camp. What was his name?"

"Evan." Brilliant, handsome, charming Evan had lit up her life like a bolt of summer lightning before leaving for Sudan and plunging her world into darkness. That they'd fought before he'd left added another layer to her misery. Fresh tears spilled over Chloe's lower lashes and she grabbed another tissue from the box on the maple dresser.

Esme sat Chloe on the bed and put an arm around her. "Is the baby Evan's? There was something about him I didn't like. He was a little too glib, if you ask me."

"You only met him once, so that's hardly fair." Wearily, Chloe shrugged her lace-covered shoulders. "I don't know whose baby I'm carrying. Daniel and I spent only one night together, but it could also be his."

Dependable, solid Daniel, a man of few words and kind deeds. She couldn't have found anyone more different than Evan, if she'd tried. After that first impetuous night with Daniel she'd leaned on him, taking comfort in his steady companionship. In the months following Evan's departure, however, it was hard not to compare Daniel's predictable ways to Evan's quick-silver charm.

Esme rubbed Chloe's back as if she were comforting a young child. "You don't have to have the baby. Aside from the question of paternity, it'll put a crimp in your ballet career. You've worked hard for years and you're finally a soloist."

Chloe twisted the tissue into a knot in her hands. "When I think of Evan traveling across the world to save other children's lives, how could I do that? I want this baby, Mom. I really do."

"But you shouldn't marry Daniel if you don't love him," Esme argued. "It's not fair to him."

"He knows I don't love him—not in the way I feel about Evan. He says that what matters is for the baby to have a mom and a dad. I like Daniel a lot, Mom. He's really good to me. And he wants the baby, even if it isn't his."

"What if Evan comes back?"

Chloe sniffed and dabbed at her nose. "He didn't want to get engaged or make any sort of promise. Two years *is* a long time, but I thought what we had was special. The worst part is we didn't make up before he left. I wrote him twice—once to tell him about the baby, and then to let him know I was getting married.

"He didn't reply to either of my letters. I kept

hoping he'd show up in time to stop the wedding." She drew in a deep breath and then let it out. "I guess it's too late now."

"Regardless of Evan, it's not too late to back out," Esme urged. "It would be hard on Daniel, but he would understand. You could come back home for a while, and your father and I would help with the baby. Marriage is a commitment you shouldn't make unless you're one hundred percent happy about it."

Chloe shook her head. "I can't. You should have seen Daniel's face when I told him I was pregnant. He was so happy, you'd think we'd planned it."

When her mother started to protest, Chloe added quickly, "It's not just for his sake that I agreed to get married. My baby deserves a father, and I know Daniel will make a good one." She tugged at the tissue, and it fell apart in her hands. "I'll never have another love like Evan, and so I might as well do what's best for my child."

"Well, if that's really what you want..." Esme's loving face softened into a thoughtful smile. "Maybe the baby will bring you and Daniel together."

"That's what he said." Chloe twisted the diamond ring—more than Daniel could afford—that weighed down her left hand. "I hope you're right."

Esme held her daughter's tight. "Daniel's a fine man. I'm sure you'll grow to love him."

A horn honked on the street below. Daniel was forgotten as Chloe ran to the window, every fantasy she'd entertained over the past month rushing to the surface. *Evan was here to stop the wedding and whisk her away. He wanted her baby, even if it wasn't his; he loved her more than life itself.*

The car outside was a white stretch limousine.

Feet sounded on the stairs. Jasmine, Chloe's best friend and maid of honor, hurried in, her dark curls bouncing above a pale blue taffeta gown. "Your father's here to take us to the church."

Reality settled like a cloak of chain mail around Chloe's shoulders, pulling her back to earth. Slowly she turned away from the window. There would be no last-minute romantic escape. She was marrying Daniel Bennett and that was that.

Blinking away her tears, she smiled and did her best to inject a lightness into her voice. "Here comes the bride."

Daniel's heart overflowed with joy and relief as he watched Chloe follow her bridesmaids in a slow procession down the aisle. Contrary to his fears, she hadn't backed out at the last minute. In her shimmering dress, with burnished hair piled high, she looked like a princess. He tried to catch her eye, but her attention was fixed on the altar.

Daniel's gaze dropped to Chloe's stomach, which was hidden by a bouquet of freesias and white roses. "Who gets married these days just because the girl is pregnant?" Rob, his brother and best man, had asked.

Daniel's answer had been simple, "*I* do."

How was it possible to love a woman as much as he loved Chloe, when she didn't love him back? He hadn't been looking for a wife; he was just a carpenter working on the construction of new homes, without a thought for the future. He'd taken his dirty clothes to the Laundromat and there she'd been, weeping over another man's dirty shirt.

Rob thought he was a sap for getting involved with a woman on the rebound, but Daniel didn't care. Chloe's relationship with Evan was over—she'd told him so. Daniel had never met anyone like her. Small and bright, lively and graceful, she reminded him of a robin, vivid red against a snow-covered fence, a sure sign that spring was on its way.

He hadn't intended to drink quite so much that first night. He'd simply tagged along to look out for her while she drowned her sorrows, but she'd insisted he match her glass for glass. Even then, it had been she who had pulled him into bed—not that he'd put up any resistance.

Daniel glanced around the packed church, which was filled with smiling, happy people. Dozens of his relatives were there, and Chloe had also invited numerous friends. Guests who couldn't find seats stood in a throng behind the back pew. There, a blond man with a three-day beard and rumpled black shirt caught Daniel's eye. Alone, among the many guests, this man was scowling.

Daniel's uneasy gaze moved back to Chloe. She was almost at the head of the aisle, gripping her father's arm with white knuckles. Then she took her place beside Daniel. Daniel's fingers curled into his palms, but he kept his smile steady and his gaze loving. No one was forcing her to marry him. Sure, she had doubts; that was understandable. That's why she needed him to be strong, certain.

The ceremony was brief, but to Daniel at least it was full of meaning. The solemn words and religious ritual sanctified their union, assured him that this marriage was meant to be. The legal bond gave him rights. The child gave him responsibilities. Chloe gave him... Well, Chloe had given him herself. And he intended to keep her.

"I do." She smiled at him, her voice tremulous but sincere.

"I do." His fingers shook as he slid the wedding band onto her finger.

Daniel kissed his bride. It was brief but, oh, so sweet. A surge of love and a fierce desire to protect and cherish her welled up in Daniel as he smiled into her eyes. Then they turned as one and walked down the aisle. The flowers decorating the pews gave off a heady scent. Chloe's hand felt small and cold nestled inside Daniel's, like a wounded bird seeking refuge.

He glanced sideways at her clean, sharp profile and his heart soared. The baby would complete the job the ceremony had begun and bind them with love and purpose.

Then he became aware of movement among the guests to his left. The blond man in the black shirt was edging his way to the front. Chloe noticed him a split second later. Daniel felt her hand tighten in his, heard her faint gasp. Evan, her ex-lover. Chloe's step faltered. Daniel supported her elbow and bore her out the door and down the steps. *Away,* he had to get her away.

They had almost reached the waiting limo when she glanced over her shoulder. Her entire being strained backward and Daniel read the terrible truth in Chloe's eyes, as a blizzard of confetti swirled around them.

She still loved Evan. He wondered if she always would.

Evan prowled the perimeter of the reception hall like a wolf circling a rival's territory. He was the un-invited guest and he felt like howling. He'd come straight from the airport—his unpacked suitcase was still in the trunk of his rental car. His fingers rubbed against the stubble on his jaw. He hadn't even taken time to shave.

Chloe and her new husband were seated at the brightly lit head table, looking as stiff as the plastic figurines atop the wedding cake. Chloe's eyes followed Evan's progress around the room, tethering him to the hall with her longing. The groom was aware of Evan, too, and his dark eyes smoldered with anger and resentment.

Why had she tied herself to this doltish lumber-jack of a man, Evan wondered. She'd moved toward that altar as if she were a virgin on her way to be sacrificed. Her nearly illegible note, dashed off in haste and smudged with her tears, had explained that she was pregnant. *Whose baby was it?*

Evan picked a glass of champagne off the tray of a passing waiter. *Was* theirs a once-in-a-lifetime love, as Chloe had maintained? Certainly his feelings for her were strong enough to make him catch the first flight out of Khartoum after receiving her letter. That had surprised even him but, then, he was always prepared, physically and mentally, for a quick departure.

The happy couple were getting up to dance the first waltz together. Evan tilted back his champagne, downing it in a long swallow that made his nose burn. Traditional claptrap, this had to be the groom's doing. Chloe was a free spirit.

A hand slid over Evan's forearm and he turned to see an attractive brunette in a red dress. "I'm Valerie," the woman said. "Would you like to dance?"

Evan started to decline—he wasn't fit company for anyone tonight. Then he glanced toward the dance floor again and set his glass on the nearest table. "It would be my pleasure."

He remembered to smile at his partner and tried to reply to her small talk, but his gaze kept drifting to Chloe. Her face, with its fine bones and eyes the color of the summer sky at twilight, was more memorable than beautiful. Although she was small, she held her back straight and her head fiercely upright. Her steps were deliberate and graceful. Her eyes were puffy, however, as if she'd been crying.

Two dances later, Evan thanked Valerie and turned to face Chloe. With a self-mocking smile and a stiff bow, he said, "My best wishes to the happy couple."

"You weren't invited..." the big man began.

"Oh, but I was," Evan said, his voice grating slightly with the effort of being civil. "Chloe sent me a letter."

"Daniel," Chloe said, holding his arm. "This is Evan."

"Who cares?" Daniel growled.

"I don't expect *you* to," Evan replied evenly. Then he turned to Chloe and asked, "May I have this dance?"

Daniel glared at him and touched Chloe on the elbow, a gesture that was both possessive and protective. "Don't."

"It's okay, Daniel," Chloe said, taking a deep breath as if to calm herself. "I'll see you back at the table."

By sheer coincidence, the next song was a ballad that Evan and Chloe had first heard together. Evan drew her into his arms and pressed his lips against her temple, not caring who saw them or what anyone thought.

"Evan, don't," she said, resisting his embrace.

"Chloe, love," he murmured. "What have you done?"

She leaned away from him to search his face. "I thought you weren't going to come." Her voice broke. "You came too late."

There was no point now in hurting her. Evan had watched the entire ceremony, including the part where the minister had asked if there was any reason why Chloe and Daniel shouldn't be joined together. The impulse to speak had been there, but only fleetingly. Evan had told her before he'd left for Sudan that he'd be back when his stint was up—and probably that would have been true. But they'd known each other a mere six weeks and he was only twenty-eight; he had a whole world to explore before he settled down.

"I'll regret that for the rest of my life." He cupped her chin with his long fingers and lifted it so he could search her eyes. "*Is* the baby mine?"

"I'm not sure," she said, her gaze sliding sideways.

A surge of irrational anger ran through him. "You got over me awfully quickly."

"I wrote to you twice," she shot back. "You didn't answer."

"It's not a sedate suburban clinic over there," he said tersely. "People are dying by the thousands."

They continued to dance in silence for a few minutes, tense at first but then gradually she relaxed and let him draw her closer. "Is hubby taking you on a honeymoon to some romantic destination?"

"We're not going anywhere," she told him. "Daniel has to work."

Evan raised their joined hands to brush his lips across her knuckles. "My return flight isn't until the end of the week. While hubby's away, Chloe could play."

Her gaze locked with his and heat rose between them. For two cents he'd drag her out of this hall and say to hell with her husband, to hell with Sudan.

"I'm *married*," she whispered. "Daniel's a good man. I can't betray him."

Evan felt a sharp stab of pain over what he'd lost. He almost felt as if he'd been betrayed. He'd been careless with women's feelings before, but no one had ever mattered to him the way Chloe did. Until this moment he hadn't even realized how strong his feelings were for her. "Paul Bunyan over there might be your lawful husband," he said, "but you'll always belong to me."

"Oh, Evan, this is such a mess." She sighed. "I love you, but I can't..." Her voice trailed off.

"You could if you wanted to." At that, her mouth pressed into a thin, stubborn line, and Evan knew he wasn't going to get his own way tonight. To his dismay, his voice shook as he asked, "Before I go may I kiss the bride?"

She nodded and he lowered his mouth to hers in a brief kiss that was achingly sweet and salted by tears. Evan cradled Chloe in his arms, lost in emotion and not knowing how he'd gotten that way.

A large hand grasped his arm, pulling Evan back. Damn, it was the glowering lumberjack. Evan cast a last glance at Chloe, and then released her. "She's all yours, mate," he said roughly to Daniel. "For now."

Chapter 2

*B*ubbles streamed from the mouthpiece of Daniel's regulator and cold water seeped into his wet suit. After an awkward duck dive he hauled himself hand over hand down the rocky underwater slope. Evan descended in an effortless glide, with an occasional casual flip of his fins. The bastard made it look so easy.

The sound of his own rasping breath and thudding heart filled Daniel's silent world. Then, as he went deeper and the pressure increased, he gained speed. Starfish and anemones slid past, barely noticed. Twenty feet, thirty feet... With too many weights on his belt, he was going too fast. He banged his knee on a rocky outcropping. The underwater flashlight strapped to his calf clanked against rocks.

Daniel fumbled for the hose of his buoyancy compensator and spurted compressed air into the vest, slowing his descent. Relief flooded his veins and he realized he was sweating despite the cold.

At the base of the slope, hovering in a cloud of sediment that rose up from the soft ocean floor, Evan waited patiently, his upturned face pale inside his mask. Anger surged through Daniel at the thought he'd allowed himself to be goaded into this expedition; had allowed this man access to his family. Daniel should be pummeling the brilliant Dr. Cutler, not trying to prove he was the man's equal.

At the bottom Daniel was still breathing heavily, and he consciously tried to slow his oxygen intake. Eyebrows raised, Evan put his thumb and forefinger together in the universal sign, waiting for Daniel's answer to the question of whether everything was okay.

Everything was not okay. His wife was in love with this man and she was probably, right this minute, planning to go away with him. Daniel formed his fingers into a circle in response. Okay.

Inside, he seethed.

Chloe unbuttoned her blouse and pushed aside her nursing bra. Six-month-old Brianna latched eagerly on to the exposed nipple and started to suck. Her sturdy little legs in their pink sleeper pushed against the arm of the chair and a tiny hand clutched at Chloe's breast.

Outside, cold November rain was falling for the

fifth day in a row, making Chloe feel like a prisoner in her own home. The rental house was small and shabby, the living room dim even in midafternoon. It was all so dreary!

Chloe stroked her daughter's downy cheek and peace settled over her, wrapping the two of them in a cocoon. Now and then Brianna stopped sucking, making small gusty sighs that caused Chloe to smile. Any hardship, any sorrow, was endurable for Brianna's sake but, oh, she missed the modern light-filled apartment overlooking the water that she'd lived in before she was married.

She'd just switched the baby to her other breast when she heard Daniel's truck pull into the gravel driveway at the side of the house. The back door opened and his boots clunked heavily on the rubber mat just inside.

Daniel padded through the living room on his way to the bedroom. Noticing Chloe, he stopped. "Why are you sitting in the dark?" he asked, flipping on the lamp.

Chloe blinked against the light. "You're home early."

"Can't work in this rain." Beads of water glistened in his black hair, which was messy from being pushed out of his eyes. "We're raising the roof trusses and it's too dangerous, even with scaffolding."

He bent to kiss the top of her head. Chloe glanced up and saw his gaze on her bare breast, and she tried, without appearing obvious, to cover herself.

Daniel pretended not to notice and gently touched the back of Brianna's hand with a fingertip. The baby stopped sucking to smile at him. "Do you want some tea?" he asked Chloe, keeping his eyes averted.

"Yes, please," she responded, feeling contrite and resentful at the same time. His love made her feel guilty, because she didn't reciprocate it. They'd both known what they were getting into when they'd decided to marry, but somehow the reality had turned out to be different from the theory.

Daniel put on the kettle, then took Brianna away to change her diaper. Chloe pulled her clothing back together and went out to the kitchen to finish making the tea. As she rinsed out the teapot in the chipped enamel sink, she felt the floorboard sag beneath her feet and looked down to see water seeping between the worn green linoleum and the baseboard.

"Daniel," she called. "We've got a problem!"

He appeared in the doorway with Brianna in his arms and watched Chloe bounce up and down on the soggy boards. "This place is a piece of crap," he said, disgusted. "We can't have Brianna crawling around in here."

"This wouldn't be happening, if we'd stayed in my apartment," Chloe couldn't help but say.

"We couldn't afford your apartment—as I explained when we went over our budget," Daniel replied patiently. "Here, we'll have a backyard for Brianna to play in next summer."

Chloe sighed as she dropped tea bags into the pot

and poured boiling water over top. She supposed Daniel was right, but next summer seemed a million years away. "I'll call the landlord. If we're lucky he'll get someone in before the weekend."

"Don't bother," Daniel said, getting an arrowroot cookie out of the tin for Brianna. "I'll fix it myself and ask for a reduction in rent."

Chloe's eyebrows rose. She still wasn't used to being with a man who could not only build a house from the ground up but who could fix anything that was broken. She poured the tea, and then carried steaming mugs into the living room.

Daniel was sitting on the floor with Brianna. After a moment's hesitation, Chloe lowered herself to the carpet to join them, tucking in one leg in and stretching out the other. Brianna sat between Chloe and Daniel, slightly wobbly but holding herself up. Chloe handed her a squeaky toy and the little girl pressed on the plastic dog with both hands, trying to make it squeak.

Daniel sipped his tea. "What did you do today?"

"Laundry, cleaning… The usual stuff." Chloe pressed her fingers into her stomach and felt the muscles that had gone soft with disuse and stretching during her pregnancy. If she was dancing they would soon tighten up again, but she wasn't going back—at least not right away. They couldn't afford child care and, anyway, she wanted to be home with Brianna. "The Joffrey Ballet is in town from New York. If my mother can baby-sit, do you want to go?"

Daniel snorted. "Pay all that money to watch a bunch of guys in tights? No, thanks."

Chloe glanced away, stung by his dismissive tone and remembering the performance she'd attended with Evan, the week before he'd left. Afterward, they'd discussed the story behind the dance and talked about how skillfully the dancers had interpreted it.

Silence descended on the room, the only sound the beating of the rain on the roof and Brianna's soft babbling. The tot banged her play dog on the carpet, finally eliciting a tiny squeak. Not satisfied with this, however, she twisted around and offered the toy to her father.

Daniel made the dog squeak and Brianna gurgled happily, displaying a gummy grin with two small bottom teeth. Then Daniel growled and tickled Brianna's tummy with the plaything. She convulsed in a belly laugh, her bright blue gaze darting between Chloe and Daniel as if inviting them both to share in her delight.

"She's really alert, isn't she?" Daniel's voice was full of pride.

Chloe smiled warmly at Daniel, her undercurrent of disappointment forgotten with their mutual adoration of Brianna. "You should have seen her today, picking up blocks and putting them in a bucket. She wore a little frown of concentration, so serious and so cute."

Brianna spied a ball behind the couch and hoisted herself onto her hands and knees, rocking back and forth as if getting ready to launch herself across the room.

Daniel grabbed the ball and placed it a foot away. Brianna edged forward. "Chloe, look, she's crawling. That's my girl!"

Chloe chuckled as Brianna reached for the ball and collapsed on her tummy. Noting the pride and pleasure on Daniel's face, she thought about his choice of words—"that's my girl." "We could get a DNA test," she said, broaching the delicate subject, which Daniel always seemed to want to avoid. "Then you'd know for sure if she was yours."

"She already *is* mine."

"I know, but…"

"I don't need proof," Daniel insisted. "I couldn't love her any more if I'd given birth to her myself."

Chloe smiled, relieved. "Okay."

Daniel placed a hand on Chloe's outstretched leg and began to massage her calf with his rough calloused fingers. For a moment Chloe just thought about how good it felt. But then she saw his dark eyes heat and she tensed and looked away, not wanting to encourage him. Daniel's smile faded as he withdrew his hand. The warmth that had built between them over Brianna suddenly cooled.

Chloe felt sick at the hurt and anger she could see in Daniel's eyes, but she couldn't help her feelings. Before Brianna was born she'd responded to Daniel's lovemaking as warmly as she could, considering how she still felt about Evan. Recovering from the birth had given her a brief reprieve, but now Daniel clearly wanted to resume their previous intimacy. At night in bed she sensed his need—as he moved restlessly in his sleep beside her and awoke each morning with an erection. She could see his frustration as he'd turn his naked body away from her and head to the bathroom for a long shower.

Chloe *wanted* to be a good wife to Daniel. Sex was part of that, but it was hard for her when she wasn't in love with him. She liked being cuddled and she enjoyed the warmth and safety of being wrapped in his strong arms. Daniel had been her friend before he became her husband, and she appreciated it. But now it seemed they were losing even that.

Chloe got to her feet and went to the window. The rain still poured down steadily, shrouding them in a silver curtain. If only she could take Brianna for a walk—anything to get out of the house. But the weather wasn't going to lift.

She watched the red mail truck slowly progress up the street, making frequent stops at the closely set houses. Outside their gate the driver jumped out in his raincoat and boots and leaned across a big puddle to push an envelope and flyers though the slot in the box.

Chloe caught a glimpse of blue—an airmail letter? Her heart leaped wildly. She'd told Evan not to write; there was no point now that she was married. But she didn't know anyone else who would send her a letter from overseas. "Mail's here."

"I'll go." Daniel started to get up. "You stay here where it's dry."

"No!" she said, quickly adding, "I need to get out of the house. For some fresh air."

Before he could protest, she threw on her raincoat and boots and splashed down the path to the front gate. Putting her body between the letterbox and the window, she leafed through the flyers for the pale blue envelope. Evan's handwriting jumped out at her, as did the Sudanese stamp and Arabic script. Stifling the impulse to pirouette in her rubber boots, she bounced on her toes and grinned foolishly. Raindrops were soaking the thin paper, so she quickly folded the letter and shoved it into the front pocket of her jeans.

Hurrying back inside, Chloe was torn between wanting to run to the bathroom to read Evan's message and knowing she had to go back to the living room and talk to Daniel as if nothing had happened.

"Any mail?" Daniel called.

Chloe stood in the doorway. "Just some flyers."

"Let's see." As she walked across to hand him the flyers, his gaze dropped to her pocket.

She glanced down involuntarily. Damp splotches darkened the faded denim. Swiftly she picked up Brianna and started to move away.

"Nothing else?" Daniel's voice was deceptively casual.

Her back to him, Chloe surprised herself when she was able to answer lightly, "No."

It was the first time she'd ever lied to Daniel—a stupid lie since he'd already caught her out. The letter from Evan in her pocket made her feel as if she had a scarlet *A* emblazoned on her forehead. She knew she was wrong to cling to the memory of Evan but between Daniel and Brianna, she had no life of her own any more. Couldn't she have this one reminder of her old life?

"Chloe?" Daniel said softly.

"I'm going to put Brianna down for her nap," she said, ignoring his unspoken plea. "Then I'll have a bath."

She tucked in Brianna and left the little girl murmuring softly to herself, then went to run a bath. Lavender-scented bath oil mingled with the stream of gushing water, filling the room with fragrant steam. Her blood humming in her veins, Chloe locked the door and stripped off her clothes.

She slit open the letter with a nail file, then eased herself into the tub, taking care not to get water on the flimsy writing paper. Banging erupted in the kitchen, followed by Daniel's muttered cursing. Chloe frowned at the closed door, worried the outburst would wake Brianna. She waited, tense and listening, until the noise abated.

Darling Chloe, she read, as she sank a little lower in the hot scented water. *I'm writing this by flashlight, as the generators have been turned off for the night. I know you told me not to write, but I can't help myself. Your photo is among my few personal possessions on the wooden crate next to the army cot that is my bed.*

You must have had your baby by now. Did your labor go all right? Does the baby look like you? Girl or boy? Not a day goes by that I don't berate myself for being halfway around the world when you needed me.

We're working sixteen-hour days in the most appalling conditions. The only thing that makes life bearable is the human contact. Jumma, the young Darfur boy who runs errands between the operating tent and the doctor's quarters, regularly has us in stitches.... Evan went on to relate a series of anecdotes that had Chloe alternately smiling and shaking her head. The world he described, while unimaginably dreadful, also contained glimpses of humor and humanity. It took her far away from her mundane round of diapers and 2:00 a.m. feedings and the daily routine of making dinner for a husband who, although kind and loving, didn't know Nureyev from Nabokov.

Finally, Evan concluded, *Remember how we talked all night and made love at dawn? I still get excited just thinking of you. I'm consumed with jealousy, knowing that someone else has his hands on your lovely body. Someday, somehow, I swear we'll be together again. Till then, thoughts of you dance like a butterfly upon my heart. Adieu, sweet Chloe. Forever yours, Evan.*

Chloe lay back in the water, the hand holding the letter dangling over the edge of the tub. *Oh, Evan.* She shut her eyes and could taste again his mouth on hers, feel his hands, sensitive and sure, touching her, arousing her. The letter slipped to the floor as she lost herself in memories of his lithe, strong body, like a god, like an angel. His laughter, his golden hair glinting in the sun, the sun-warmed scent of his skin... The images and feelings she created in her mind were so real that she never wanted to open her eyes.

Gradually the water cooled and reality intruded. Chloe sat up, blinking against the light, noticing the cracks in the green tiles, the black mold in the grout, the damp under-the-sink smell that never went away no matter how frequently she cleaned. Suddenly she felt weak and depressed.

Wearily she pulled herself up and looked around for the soap and a washcloth. Lathering soap onto the cloth, she started scrubbing. Tears rolled down her cheeks and fell onto her swollen breasts.

"Chloe?" Daniel's voice was right outside the door. "Are you okay?"

"I'm fine," she choked out. "I'll be out in a minute."

"I'm going to get some plywood," he said and started to open the door. "I need to wash my hands."

"Wait!" Panicking, Chloe reached for Evan's letter. Water dripped onto the tile floor and she spoke loudly to cover the rustle of paper. "Can't you do that in the kitchen?"

"We're out of soap there." He paused before curtly adding, "May I come in?"

"Just a second." Chloe shoved the letter into a drawer in the vanity. Submerging herself in the sloshing bathwater, she wrapped her arms around her bent knees. "Okay."

Daniel glanced at the puddle on the floor and then looked at Chloe in the mirror. "You should come out if you're cold."

"I will soon." Halfheartedly she splashed lukewarm water over her shoulders.

He searched the bottom cupboard. "I can't find the soap. Did you put it in a drawer?"

"It's in the cabinet," Chloe said quickly. "I'm positive."

Daniel glanced over his shoulder at her anxious tone, then moved a package of toilet paper. "You're right. Here it is." Carefully he unwrapped a bar of soap and put the paper in the trash. Even then he didn't leave.

"What is it?" Chloe asked, ready to scream.

"Are you sure you're all right?"

"Of course," she said. "Why do you keep asking that?"

His dark eyes searched her face. He shrugged and said simply, "I'll be back soon."

She waited until she heard his truck pull out, then got out of the tub. Wrapped in a towel, she removed Evan's letter from the drawer and tucked it inside a box of sanitary napkins. It was only when she was dressed and combing out her hair that she looked at the reflection of herself and saw her red-rimmed eyes.

Daniel wasn't stupid. He must have guessed she was crying over a letter from Evan. If only she could talk things over with Daniel, the way she had when they'd met. He'd been so understanding, so compassionate, counseling her not to count on a man who had gone away without making up after they'd fought. What would he advise her to do now?

How do I stop loving the man who's my kindred spirit? she imagined herself asking Daniel. *How do I start loving my husband when we have nothing in common but our child? Was I wrong to marry one man when I love another?*

But she could no longer talk to Daniel about Evan. She'd made her choice and it wasn't fair to have second thoughts. Neither could she rid her heart of Evan, even if she'd wanted to. That was her real crime—she didn't *want* to stop loving Evan.

Chloe layered on a woolen undershirt and one of Daniel's thick flannel workshirts, drew on her heavy corduroy pants and buried her feet in socks and slippers, trying to get warm. She just had time to throw a stew together and get it simmering on the stove before Daniel returned from the building-supply outlet with sheets of plywood.

His handheld electric saw whirred, drowning out the radio Chloe'd turned on, and piece by piece he replaced the flooring. Chloe sat in the living room knitting a blanket for Brianna's crib, shutting out her thoughts with the rhythmic clicking of the needles. After Daniel finished repairing the floor, he spent the rest of the day digging a trench down one side of the house and laying drainage tiles. He worked in the pouring rain until the light was gone, before coming in soaking wet, his nose dripping and his reddened hands like ice.

"I'll run you a hot bath to warm up," Chloe said, putting down her knitting to hang up his sodden rain jacket.

Daniel gave her an oblique glance. "No, thanks."

Later she lay in bed in the dark, worrying, while she listened to Daniel brushing his teeth. A thin line of yellow light glowed around the closed bathroom door. She should have moved the letter to a safer place. She should have destroyed it. She should have…

The water stopped. The toothbrush clattered softly in the metal holder. Chloe caught her breath, her ears straining in the silence. She heard a drawer slide open slowly. More silence. Then the drawer was shut and another opened.

Daniel glanced through the contents of the drawer—hairdryer, bottles of shampoo and conditioner, a box of sanitary napkins, hairbrush. He picked up the half-empty box of napkins. If she thought he was too squeamish to look in here, she didn't know him very well. Breath held, he pushed his hand inside… *Bingo.*

Daniel withdrew the envelope and studied the address. He was an expert on Evan's bold, elegant handwriting, having seen the various cards he'd given Chloe, all of which she'd saved. There'd been a birthday card, cards with funny pictures and cards with romantic scenes, all overflowing with Evan's witty observations, references to shared experiences or poetic allusions that Daniel didn't begin to understand.

Daniel picked up the envelope and tested the solid thickness of several sheets of paper. Rage and despair flooded him as he thought about the sheer unfairness of having to compete with Evan, who used words so easily he could fill pages and pages with them. Daniel's hand started to tighten around the envelope. Hastily he stuffed it back into the box before he ended up crumpling it into a ball. Quietly, carefully, he shut the drawer. He didn't need to read the letter to know Evan had once again seduced Chloe.

Daniel had hoped that when they were married and Evan was gone again that part of Chloe's life would be over. Now he realized it would never be over, as long as Evan continued to occupy a place in her mind and her heart. Daniel had married Chloe because he wanted to do right by her and the baby and because, God help him, he loved her.

Had they made a terrible mistake? He couldn't say. All he knew was that, where Brianna was concerned, he'd done the only thing he could have done. Right or wrong became irrelevant when weighed against the bone-deep love he felt for the child. The only thing that gave him hope was the knowledge that Chloe felt the same about their daughter.

Daniel put his dirty clothes in the wicker hamper and folded his towel on the rack. Then, so he wouldn't wake Chloe, he turned out the light and went to bed in the dark, feeling his way along the wall until his knee bumped the bedside table.

Once under the covers he was tormented by the warmth and scent of the woman in his bed. Usually he kept his distance, huddled on his side so he wouldn't accidentally touch her thigh or brush against her breast and end up tossing and turning all night. Tonight repressed desire made him reach for her, and he wanted to possess her. He felt her tense, but he shifted closer to kiss her neck. "Chloe."

She started to squirm away. "Daniel, I…"

He took her mouth before she could tell him to stop, plunging his tongue inside with a ruthlessness that further inflamed him. His hand found her breast and the blood roared in his ears. She started to kiss him back and her pelvis pressed against him so that he groaned aloud. *At last.* She wanted him, too.

"You're beautiful, like a…a goddess," he muttered clumsily, struggling to be the kind of man she longed for. "I want you more than a flower wants the sun, more than…" More than he could say, he thought disparagingly. He gave up and pressed his lips to her cheek and along her nose to her soft fluttering eyelashes. There he encountered moisture and tasted salt. Damn. She was crying.

"I'm s-sorry, Daniel," she stuttered. "I...I can't."

His taut skin strained with a physical pain and his fingers dug into the soft flesh of her upper arm. A single word exploded from him. *"When?"*

She shrank back. "I don't know."

Daniel threw himself onto his back and flung an arm over his eyes, rigid in a red haze of thwarted desire. After a moment he became aware of her sharply drawn breaths and irregular hiccups. "Come here," he said gruffly and pulled her into his arms.

She went with a soft sigh. "I'm sorry."

"Never mind," he said heavily, smoothing her hair away from her face. "It doesn't matter."

"Maybe I could do it if..."

Hope surged and was quickly checked. Cautiously, he asked, "If what?"

"If you didn't *want* me so much."

At first he was confused. She didn't want him to want her? How could they make love if he wasn't aroused? Then he realized—she didn't want him to need her emotionally. No words of love, no adoration or expectations. Just animals fulfilling their physical needs.

"I told you when I proposed, that I wouldn't ask for more than you can give, and I stand by it," he said quietly. He hadn't realized at the time that not being able to express his love would be the price he was going to pay for her hand in marriage.

"Okay, then." She turned to him awkwardly, a little shyly, and put her arms around his neck.

Daniel kissed her tentatively, trying not to pour all the bittersweet love he felt in his heart into a deep embrace that would make her withdraw again. Beneath her flannelette nightgown her skin was smooth and satiny, her muscles sleek and firm. Soon he forgot everything but the need to sink himself into her softness. He tugged the fabric up past her waist and over her head, gazing down at her. He could just make out the faint shine of her eyes. *Don't cry, babe.*

Chloe bit her lip as she gazed up at him. "Please don't be upset if I don't come." Quickly, she added, "It's not that you're not attractive or a good lover, it's just that…"

Daniel pressed his fingers to her lips, silencing her. "Just don't talk for a while." He'd taken enough blows to his pride for one day.

He used a condom, even though she was breast-feeding and even though it was like locking the barn door after the horse had bolted. The last thing they needed was another accident. He was as tender as he could be and drew out the lovemaking as long as he could manage. But he'd wanted Chloe so badly and for so long that he came more quickly than he'd have wished. Just as she'd predicted, she didn't climax.

When he'd recovered sufficiently, he lifted himself

onto his elbows and kissed her damp eyelids. "Do you want me to…"

"*No,*" she said swiftly. "Thank you."

Stung by her politeness as much as her rejection, Daniel drew himself out of her and rolled onto his back. Well, he'd known what the score was, because she'd told him. When was he going to figure it out? She didn't want him. Didn't need him. Didn't damn well love him.

"Daniel?" She slipped one arm over his chest and snuggled into his side. "Let's just hold each other."

Daniel fought back his disappointment to savor having her in his arms, because just holding her satisfied another need as deep as sex. And who knew, tomorrow she might regret this intimacy and insist they go back to being husband and wife in name only.

After a few minutes' silence, he said, "There's a piece of waterfront property out past Sooke being subdivided."

"Oh?" she replied, yawning sleepily.

"I'm building a house for the developer." He stroked her hair, thinking how soft it was, like…like… "I want to buy one of the lots. The developer will do a straight trade, if I build his house for cost. After that, I'll build a house for us. I've worked out the finances and it's a stretch, but I think we can just manage."

She'd been half-asleep in his arms, but suddenly there was a wakeful alertness to her. "A house for us?"

"It's isolated," he said quickly, "but I know you miss your view of the water and I've always loved the ocean. When we're a bit more secure financially, we'll get a second car for you. It would be good to have our own place."

She was quiet for such a long time that he thought she'd fallen asleep, but when he turned to look, her eyes were wide open staring at the ceiling. He didn't even want to ask what she was thinking. "Sleep on it," he suggested.

"No, let's just do it." She spoke quietly but with a kind of grim determination.

Perhaps her lack of enthusiasm ought to have discouraged him, but instead the flickering flame of hope flared back to life. He kissed her temple and said, "I'll call the owner in the morning."

Someday, he vowed, she was going to love him as much as he loved her. As his eyes closed, a more sobering thought filtered through. Before that day came, how many times would she have to consciously choose him before he believed she intended to stay?

Chapter 3

The weight of the water pulled Daniel down. Sixty, then eighty feet; deeper than he'd ever gone before. The pressure glued his wet suit to his skin and sucked his mask against his face. It was cold and dark and eerily silent.

Evan left the rocks that marked the shoreline and moved out over the flat muddy sand of the ocean floor. Daniel forced himself to follow across the featureless landscape as visibility faded into murky darkness. The bottom sloped gently down. Every now and then one of Evan's fins kicked up a cloud of silt, obscuring Daniel's view of him.

Where were the other divers? Daniel twisted awkwardly in his bulky suit and constraining scuba gear, but he couldn't see anyone else. He and Evan might be the only two people left on the planet. Wouldn't that be fine? Trapped in a twilight zone of gloom with the one man in his life he could truly say he hated.

Damn Evan. He was swimming too fast, getting too far ahead. He was just a dim shape, a blur of blue neoprene against the dark sepia tones of the deep. How convenient if he "lost" Daniel down here. He'd be sure to comfort the poor widow. Would she grieve or would she secretly be glad?

Daniel checked his depth gauge—100 feet. This place gave him the creeps. For two cents, he'd surface right now. Except that Chloe would look at him with that sympathetic glance of hers, the one she used when she was trying to be comforting. She wouldn't blame him for aborting the dive, but that was no consolation. Didn't she know that a man didn't want pity from his woman? He wanted respect, admiration, adoration. All the things he had always seen in her eyes when she looked at Evan.

Well, he wouldn't beg for her love. That was one thing he'd decided on early in their marriage. She either loved him or she didn't, but he would never demean himself by pleading for her affection.

Evan was completely out of sight now. Daniel fumbled for his flashlight, his fingers clumsy in the thick three-fingered mitts. Finally he felt the recessed button respond and a yellow beam illuminated an unexpected scene.

Rising from the sea floor not ten feet away were a dozen or so sea pens, their feathery bright orange fronds waving gently in the current like so many dyed ostrich plumes. He knew what they were from the book of underwater sea life

Brianna had given him last Christmas, but he'd never thought he'd see such an amazing sight with his own eyes.

He swam over to them. After a few minutes of intense observation, he reached out to the delicate curling tentacles. At his touch, water squirted from the central stalk and the colony of animals that made up the pen deflated and sank into the sand. Surprised, Daniel kicked backward.

And bumped into Evan, coming to find him. Evan saw the sea pens and his mouth curved in an appreciative smile around his regulator. For a moment they were united by a common interest. For a moment Daniel forgot his antipathy. Then he remembered. That mouth that smiled in camaraderie had kissed Chloe, the hand that motioned him to "come on" had touched his wife intimately, the eyes that met his had looked upon her naked body.

He and Evan might be dive buddies, but they were about as far from being friends as two men could get.

"Close your eyes." Daniel held Chloe by the hand and led her up the steps. Piles of offcuts and concrete rubble lay here and there, and the yard was bare dirt, but their new home was ready to move into.

"I've walked every inch of this house at every stage of construction," Chloe said, with a little laugh over his excitement. "I've picked out tiles and carpets and paint colors. Why close my eyes now?"

"Just do it," Daniel urged, turning a key in the lock. This was his moment and he wanted it to be perfect.

Chloe closed her eyes, then immediately opened

them. "What about Brianna? We can't leave her in the car."

"She's fast asleep," Daniel reminded her. "The car's parked in front of the garage, with the U-Haul truck right behind. She'll be all right for a minute. *Now close your eyes.*"

Chloe obeyed. A moment later she let out a whoop as Daniel scooped her into his arms. "Keep them shut," he warned, nudging the door open with his hip and carrying her across the threshold.

Chloe clung to his neck, shrieking a bit with every unexpected lurch. She felt like a wisp of nothing in his arms even though he'd seen the muscles in her thighs as she balanced on her toes. It was easy to forget how much strength was needed for her dancing.

The first time he'd seen her glide across a stage she'd reminded him of a sleek sea bird skimming over the waves. He'd wanted to shelter her, so he'd built a nest for her and their chick, combining those elements that held meaning for him—sky and sea, a cozy haven, a dwelling place for love.

Chloe would cringe with embarrassment if Daniel were to reveal his clumsy poetic thoughts. So he simply walked into the great room and stood with his back to the wide, tall windows high above the Strait of Juan de Fuca. He wanted her first sight to be the family room and kitchen, the heart of the house. "You can open your eyes now."

Chloe slid out of his arms and gazed silently at the gleaming appliances and terra-cotta tiles, the warm

Mediterranean colors. She turned slowly in a circle, past the breathtaking view, the built-in teak shelving and the stone fireplace, and back to Daniel. Solemn and silent, she seemed about to cry. "You did this."

"Not all by myself." There was an enormous lump in his throat. "Do you like it?"

"Oh, Daniel, it's beautiful." She put her arms around him, her words muffled by his shirt. "I knew what it was going to look like, but until now it was almost unreal—as if someone else was going to live here. I can't believe it's ours. You are amazing."

Daniel held her, then reluctantly eased himself away. "I'll go check on Brianna. You look around some more."

"Wait." Chloe slid a hand up his chest and curled her fingers around his neck. Balancing on her toes, she rose up to kiss him.

Her mouth opened and her tongue shyly pressed against his, flooding him with heat. Daniel gathered her close, hiding his rush of surprise by deepening the kiss. Chloe so rarely initiated anything. With one hand cupping her buttocks, Daniel gently molded one small, firm breast. To his surprise, she didn't pull away as she so often had before, but instead reached for his belt buckle.

He glanced over his shoulder. The front door was open so they could hear Brianna if she cried out but… The front door was open.

Anyone could walk in, and the thought excited him.

"Don't worry." She was breathing heavily as she slid

his zipper down over his bulging erection. "This won't take long."

"I don't have a condom on me."

Chloe grinned up at him. "We're married, aren't we?"

A jolt of pure joy shot through Daniel. He slid his hands beneath her denim skirt and eased down her panties. She was slick and hot beneath his probing fingers. Down onto the brand-new carpet they fell in a tangled heap, Daniel's jeans halfway down his legs and Chloe's skirt up around her waist. A button popped open on her blouse, exposing a swelling curve of flesh. Daniel sucked on the rosy nipple and felt Chloe's legs spread beneath him. The submissive gesture, the giving way, *the welcoming,* flipped a switch in his brain and all the months of control slipped away as he entered her.

"Sorry," he panted, withdrawing instantly. "Too hard?"

"Harder," she said, teeth gritted, back arching.

Their coupling was short and fierce and sweet beyond measure. Afterward Daniel raised himself onto his elbows, taking his weight off her glistening body. Her eyes were closed, her smile dreamy with contentment. "So," he said. "A new house is a big turn-on for you."

Chloe tilted her head back and laughed, her slender throat vibrating. "It's *you,* you big, sweaty lug. *You're* the turn-on."

Grinning, Daniel stuck his nose into an armpit. "That good? Maybe I should bottle it."

Then her eyes opened, and Daniel was surprised to see them mist over as her laughter faded and was replaced with a tremulous smile. "Thank you, Daniel," she whispered. "You've made us a family."

"Brianna made us a family," he replied gruffly.

Chloe ran her hands over his shoulders and down his arms, tracing the hard outlines of his biceps. "*You* are the bricks and mortar, the solid foundation of our lives. I really love you."

The way she said it, she could have meant she loved him as a friend. Foolish or not, however, Daniel chose to interpret her words in the most positive way. He dipped his head to kiss her lightly on the lips. "Now *that's* something to build upon."

Daniel went out to the car and brought Brianna inside. The one-year-old rubbed her eyes and blinked sleepily at the unfamiliar surroundings. "She was just waking. If you want to take her, I'll start bringing in our boxes."

"Let's look through the house together first," Chloe said. "Decide where we want to put everything."

"That'll be an easy decision," Daniel replied. "Since we don't have much."

The design of their house was elegant in its simplicity, and above all, it was functional. All the rooms were large and spacious. Their bedroom, like the living room, faced the ocean and had its own deck. Directly across the hall was Brianna's room, then the bathroom and linen closet, and then a much larger room. Daniel had called it a rec room during construction, but now its true purpose was revealed.

Chloe stopped short in the doorway to survey the bare floorboards. "Where's the carpet?" Then she noticed the barre and the wall-to-wall floor-to-ceiling mirror.

He waited, hands clenched, for her reaction. Why the hell hadn't he discussed it with her first? He'd wanted to surprise her, that's why.

Those mirrors had cost a fortune, but damn it, he wanted to give her this. He wanted her not to regret giving up her dancing along with her lover when she'd married him.

Brianna was wriggling in his arms, so Daniel set her on the floor. She toddled into the room, saw herself in the mirror and giggled with delight. With graceful steps, Chloe took the little girl's hands and twirled her in a pirouette. She glanced over her shoulder at Daniel, her face alight. "This is wonderful. Thank you."

Daniel felt the tension seep from his shoulders and he leaned against the doorjamb, watching his girls spin and twirl. Winning Chloe's smile made the extra work and expense worthwhile. "I thought you could teach here, until you're ready to rejoin the ballet company."

Chloe's steps slowed, and she surveyed the room as she examined the possibilities in her mind. "There aren't many children around here, but Sooke isn't so far away. Teaching might be just the thing." Then she crossed the floor, to tug on his hands. "Come on, dance with us."

"I'm no good at that stuff." He loved the way Chloe celebrated life through her love of movement, but next to her he was big and clumsy.

"Yes, you are. Come on," she urged, twirling under his arm. Her clear, sweet voice lilted in a wordless melody as she encouraged him to sidestep across the room.

Daniel felt like an idiot clunking around in his heavy boots, but Chloe's smile was contagious and after a moment he laughed and gave in, hamming it up when Brianna started to clap. A rush of happiness caught him off guard. His wife had made love to him and his baby daughter adored him. Life was good. He picked up Chloe and Brianna in his arms and spun around until they were all dizzy and laughing.

Finally Chloe, gasping for breath, pounded on his shoulders. "Put me down."

Daniel stopped spinning and set them down, still smiling. "Guess we'd better get to work."

Within a couple of hours, they'd carried in the few pieces of furniture they owned—a brand-new bed with matching side tables, Brianna's crib and chest of drawers, Daniel's tallboy and a bookcase he'd had before they'd married, a couch and matching chair upholstered in maroon corduroy and a pine coffee table they'd bought at an auction. The only good piece of furniture they owned was a round oak dining table that Chloe's parents had given them as a wedding present.

"Our furniture looks a bit shabby now that it's in our new house," Daniel said when they'd arranged the pieces. "And sparse."

"It's fine," Chloe insisted, tucking her hand through his arm. "We'll have more as we go along."

Daniel covered her small hand with his larger one. In the year and a half that had passed since they'd gotten married, this was the first time she'd talked about the future with any sense of permanency.

"What's important is that it's a new beginning," Daniel said, almost to himself.

Eyes shining, Chloe turned to face him and took both his hands in hers. "Yes. A new beginning." Then her face dimmed a little and she bit her lip. "Daniel, I should tell you, I've been doing something I shouldn't. You see…"

"Don't." He squeezed her hands, not wanting to hear the words spoken aloud. "You don't need to say anything." He hadn't found any new letters in several months and he'd assumed that she'd finally gotten over the Australian doctor. He might have known for sure if he'd actually read the correspondence, but he'd refused to invade her privacy.

Her forehead creased in a worried frown. "But…"

He searched her face. "You meant it when you agreed this is a new beginning, didn't you?"

"Yes." She gazed back steadily and an understanding passed silently between them. With a tentative smile she wrapped her arms around his waist and pressed her cheek to his chest. "I swear I'll be a good wife to you."

Daniel stroked her hair, savoring the closeness. "Don't be silly. You already are. Do you want to take a walk on the beach?"

Chloe's glance shifted to the window and the bright blue sky. She hesitated and then she said, "Not right now. I'd like to unpack some of those boxes, and Brianna's going to need something to eat soon. You go."

Daniel followed the path he'd cleared on previous walks through the salal bushes down to the small beach. The coastline curved outward in either direction to a rocky point where waves surged and foamed. Here in the center of the cove, the water was calm. A breeze ruffled his hair and brought the tang of salt and seaweed close. Brianna would learn to swim here, the way he'd learned to swim on the west coast of the island near Tofino where he'd grown up. The water was cold, but that just made a person strong.

He walked along the shoreline, his boots crunching in the loose shells and gravel, stooping now and then to pick up an abalone shell and admire its opalescent inner surface. A crow flew overhead, cawing, and settled with a noisy flap of black wings high in a fir tree at the edge of the beach.

As Daniel rubbed a smooth stone between his fingers, thoughts of Chloe flitted through his mind. The sweetness of her smile, her eagerness as she surged beneath him, her passionate feelings for their new house. Just when he thought he was beginning to understand her, she surprised him. It would probably always be that way with them. The fact that she was his wife at all was still astonishing.

Daniel stopped and looked up at the house and felt his heart fill with pride and hope for the future. This was their home. His and Chloe's and Brianna's. Someday there would be more children.

He frowned and blinked. Was that a wisp of smoke coming from the fireplace chimney? Daniel stared hard for another minute, then shook his head. The sky was perfectly clear. He must have been imagining things.

Pocketing the abalone shell to show Chloe and Brianna, he headed back to the house.

Humming the celebrated pas de deux from *Swan Lake,* Chloe twirled across the kitchen floor between the fridge and Brianna's high chair, setting a small tub of yogurt on the tray with a flourish. Brianna rewarded her performance with a giggle and a clap of her sticky fingers.

"You like that?" Chloe said to her. "You should have seen me dance the solo." She mimed the dying swan princess, folding her crumpled wings and slithering to the floor where she rested motionless, collapsed. Brianna leaned over the side of her high chair, watching intently to see if her mother would rise again.

Chloe lifted her head and Brianna smiled.

"Ah, Brianna, if only…" Chloe slowly rose to her feet. If only what? Her audience wasn't a fourteen-month-old child? Her life hadn't telescoped from opening nights and nationwide appearances to diapers and vacuuming? She loved Brianna and adored the house and Daniel was an angel, but there was no point in denying that her life lacked excitement.

It had been two long months since they'd moved in. Daniel reveled in the wildness and solitude of the ocean and the forest, but Chloe missed people—especially during the work week when her friends were all busy in the city. She still missed walking out of her apartment and strolling down the street to the corner café or going out to a concert in the evening.

She was foraging through the sparse pickings in the fridge for her own lunch when the doorbell rang.

"Who could that be?" She tugged on her tank top to smooth it down and pushed back the wisps that straggled from the twist of hair at the back of her head. Her mother and father always called before they visited, and besides they only came on Sundays.

Chloe hurried down the hall to open the front door. "Oh, my God," she gasped. "What are *you* doing here?"

Chapter 4

Evan presented her with a dozen red roses wrapped in gold paper and gave her his trademark brilliant smile. "Is that any way to greet your long-lost love?"

She cradled the blooming flowers in the crook of her arm. Primly, she said, "You're not my love now."

He laughed and kissed her quickly on the mouth. A whiff of his aftershave, leather and sandalwood, caught her unaware and transported her back to the past. To a brief but intense history of tumbled beds and Sunday brunch in fine hotels, to violin concertos and kisses in the rain.

Flustered, she backed away. "I'd better put these in

water." Seeing Evan sling his canvas-and-leather satchel down inside the door, she added in alarm, "You can't stay here."

"I know that." His lighthearted Aussie drawl always made it sound to Chloe as if he were on the verge of laughter. "Your lumberjack would chop me up for kindling."

"Don't call him that," Chloe said. "Daniel's a good man."

Her heart beating rapidly, she walked briskly back to the kitchen. She could feel Evan's gaze on her bare legs and his powerful presence in her house. Daniel's house. Dropping the bouquet in the sink, she faced him. "Didn't you get my last letter?"

Evan's light blue eyes burned into hers. "The one where you told me not to write anymore?" A sound from the high chair made him glance past her shoulder. His deeply tanned skin paled. "Is this your daughter?"

"Brianna." Chloe found a tall, square vase in the cupboard and filled it with water. "She's—"

"Fourteen months old last week," Evan said. Chloe stepped aside and he walked toward the little girl who was smearing strawberry yogurt around her tray. "G'day, Brianna," he said softly. "How's it going?"

Brianna lifted a round trusting face and displayed her yogurt-covered fingers for his inspection. Evan studied her intently, then turned to Chloe. "She looks just like you." He paused. "I can't see anything of me *or* Daniel in her."

Chloe busied herself arranging the roses. "Naturally, she's like Daniel."

"So you've had a DNA test?"

He sounded disappointed. Did he really wish Brianna was his? Fear clutched at Chloe. What if he contested the issue of paternity and sued for custody? Daniel would be devastated and Brianna would be traumatized. "Y-yes, yes, we have," she faltered, not looking at him. "She's definitely Daniel's child."

Evan tipped up her chin and searched her face. "Liar."

Chloe blushed and pulled away. "All right, we haven't, but this is her home and Daniel *is* her father."

"Do you really imagine I'd try to take her away from a stable, secure family?" Evan shook his head. "What would I do with a toddler, anyway? A refugee camp is no place for a child. At least not for fortunate kids like Brianna who have a home."

"Have you finished your stint in Sudan?" Chloe rinsed a cloth in warm water and wiped Brianna's hands. Relief flooded through her. He wasn't going to upset the fragile balance she'd finally achieved in her life, in her marriage. Anyway, she wouldn't let him. "I thought you were there for two years."

"They let me off a month early for good behavior." Chloe's eyebrows rose and he admitted the truth. "I got a recurrence of malaria, a bad bout. I went to Paris to recuperate but the City of Lights isn't much fun when you're sick and on your own. So then I decided to head home, stopping on my way to visit my brother in Victoria."

"How is Jack?" she said.

"I haven't seen him yet. I came here straight from the airport." Evan moved closer and stroked his knuckles lightly down her arm. "Did you really not want my letters? Or did the lumberjack force you to put me off?"

"Don't call him that!" Chloe shivered at Evan's touch. Unsettled, she slipped sideways out of his reach. "Daniel doesn't even know about our correspondence. I made the decision to stop writing myself. In fact, I burned all your letters the day we moved here."

He winced. "That was cruel."

"You know we can't continue to have a relationship." She wrapped her arms around her waist, anchoring her fingers in the waistband of her skirt. "How did you find me at this address?"

"Your husband runs a business out of his house and he's listed in the Yellow Pages. It didn't require Sherlock Holmes to track you down." He glanced around at the warm maple cabinets and the granite countertop. "It's nice. Daniel's a good builder, I'll give him that."

"I was just going to have some lunch," she said, softening her tone a little. She went to the cupboard and took out a can of tuna. "Will you join me?"

"Yes, but put away the canned fish." He brought his satchel into the kitchen and proceeded to pull out a portable feast. "Remember how we used to talk about going to Paris?" he asked Chloe, placing a luscious circle of brie and shrink-wrapped pâté on the counter. "Since we didn't get there together, I'm bringing Paris to you. *Pain de campagne,*" he went on, handing her a heavy round loaf. "Olives. Italian, not French, but still… Dried muscatel grapes and—" with a flourish he produced a foil-capped bottle "—real Champagne."

Chloe burst into delighted laughter. "Evan, you are the limit! But this is just what I needed today." She got Brianna out of her high chair and set her on the floor with some toys. Then she cleared the newspapers and flyers off the dining table. She started to bring out the everyday plates, then changed her mind and got a stool to reach into the top cupboard for the set of good china her grandmother had given her as a wedding present. Real champagne all the way from France deserved crystal flutes.

"Do you have an ice bucket for the wine?" Evan asked.

"I have a plastic bucket in the laundry room."

For some reason this struck them both as hilarious. Suddenly a party atmosphere had taken over, as they unwrapped the food and poured the wine together. Conversation and laughter bubbled along with the champagne. Chloe ate ravenously and drank with abandon, as if this might be her last meal. She hadn't felt so alive in months. *Maybe not since Evan left,* a tiny voice whispered. She brushed the thought aside and let him refill her champagne glass. His tales of adventure ranged from Sudan to Istanbul to the glittering restaurants and theaters of Paris.

Chloe took in his chiseled features and golden hair. His thin V-necked cashmere sweater looked sophisticated and sexy over designer blue jeans. She watched his long fingers restlessly toy with the cutlery. Fingers that had brought her unparalleled pleasure had also saved lives and comforted the sick.

"What was it like in the refugee camp?" she asked. "It must have been awful."

Shadows filled his eyes, hinting at never-to-be-forgotten scenes of horror. "It's like nothing you can imagine. Hell on earth. Patients arrive in a continuous stream, and the suffering is beyond imagining— limbs hacked off, women raped almost to the point of death, mutilated children, disease, starvation... We do what we can, minute by minute, hour by hour, day by day, but there's no respite.

"Horrible as that is, I could cope with it. But it's what I *couldn't* do that tormented me, the hundreds of people I had to turn away because the clinic simply didn't have the resources to treat them all." He tilted his glass to his lips, but he'd already drained it dry. "Have you got anything else to drink?"

"I'll go see." Chloe got up, staggered a little and

laughed. "I'm not used to drinking in the afternoon." She wagged her finger at him. "You're a bad influence."

"Good," he replied with a wicked grin. "You look as though you could use shaking up."

"I do not!" she said hotly. "I have a great life. A wonderful husband and a beautiful child."

Suddenly remembering Brianna, she glanced around the room in a panic. Her heart flooded with relief. The baby was playing quietly with her activity center. Feeling her mother's gaze on her, Brianna looked over and raised her arms to be picked up.

"There you are, pumpkin," Chloe cooed, gathering her into her arms. "You're being such a good girl."

"Unlike her mother?" Evan drawled.

Chloe ignored that and went to the fridge with Brianna still in her arms. "There's some Chateau Cardboard," she said, eyeing a box of white wine wedged between the milk and the orange juice.

"Oh, my, you have come down in the world," Evan teased. "I suppose it's better than nothing."

Chloe felt her cheeks flush. "Or there's Glenlivet."

"That sounds better," Evan said. "A couple fingers of scotch ought to cure what ails me."

Chloe got down the bottle of expensive whiskey with a feeling of misgiving. This was Daniel's one luxury: he allowed himself a single drink before dinner on the weekends. Still, she couldn't let Evan think her marriage had dragged her down—although by comparison to *his* life her surroundings must seem boring and hopelessly provincial.

She tried to put Brianna back on the floor but the little girl cried, so Chloe put her in her high chair and cut her a hunk of the chewy country bread that Evan had brought. "That'll give your gums a workout."

Leaving Brianna to eat, Chloe poured Evan a drink. He got up from the table and came into the kitchen, where she handed it to him.

"Come on, you have to join me." He grinned. "Might as well be hanged for a sheep as a lamb."

She hesitated for a moment, then with an answering grin and a shrug she sloshed a small amount into another glass. She was just drunk enough not to worry about consequences.

Evan sipped his scotch, leaning against the counter and gazing down at her with an indulgent smile. "How have things been with you? Made lots of friends in this neck of the woods?"

"We don't have many neighbors yet. The lots haven't all sold and only one other house has been built so far—that of the man we bought the land from. His wife works, and anyway we don't have much in common. A fisherman lives down the road, but when he's not out on his boat he's in the pub."

"But you could drive into the city. Visit your old friends?"

"We don't have a second car," she explained, adding defensively, "but we will, soon. I'm going to be teaching ballet. I've printed up and distributed leaflets." She stopped herself with a small sigh. "Nothing will happen until school starts in September."

"A whole month away." Evan watched her carefully. "Your lumber… Sorry, your *husband* must be quite something to keep you satisfied out here in the sticks."

She shrugged unhappily. "He works long hours during the summer, traveling up island and even across to Saltspring Island."

"Leaving the missus all alone and lonely," Evan said softly.

"I'm not…" she started, then broke off. She *was* lonely. But that wasn't Daniel's fault. "He has to take every job he can get. Come winter, work will be scarce." The champagne and the whiskey were making Chloe confused. Did she resent Daniel for having to defend him or Evan for making her see how dull her life was? Daniel had built her this house, but then he'd left her imprisoned like a princess waiting to be rescued.

"Where is he now?" Evan reached out to tuck a tendril of her hair behind Chloe's ear. "Will he be home soon?"

"He's in Duncan. He won't be home for hours." Chloe held her breath. At the end of the U-shaped kitchen, she didn't have much room to maneuver. Evan was so close, just a touch away, and so tempting. Gazing into his sky blue eyes, she could easily imagine that she was still in love with him and he with her.

"I've missed you, Chloe," he murmured. "Missed your smile, your touch." He bent his head, his lips inches from hers. "I've been lonely, too."

Chloe started to strain toward him, then suddenly stopped herself. This was crazy. Her heart beat fast as she backed away, only to find herself hard against the counter. "You've been gone two years. You must have had other women."

"In the camp we were four to a room, with a few fitful hours of sleep a night. Not exactly a romantic setting."

"In Paris, then." He was too handsome not to attract women. And what man could resist being pursued?

Right now he was doing the pursuing, edging closer until his hips brushed hers and his hands skimmed her arms.

"Ah, French women—they're charming and chic." He captured her hand and kissed the palm. "But *we* have a connection, Chloe. Our minds work the same way. Our hearts beat as a single unit." He placed his hand below her left breast. "I can feel your heart beating now, like a small wild bird."

Chloe licked her parted lips, helpless as that wild bird to stop what was going to happen next. Nor did she want to—she craved Evan's kiss with a kind of madness. It was all she could think of; the need to feel his mouth on hers, his hands on her body.

She slid her arms around his neck and drew him

to her, hungrily tasting his lips, his tongue. So familiar, yet so exotic—a postcard of paradise, remembered and yearned after, finally within reach. The kiss went on and on, erasing her will and replacing it with feverish need. Dimly she heard a clattering, metal on tile, and couldn't make sense of the sound.

Yet a hole had been torn in the silken sensuality that Evan had wrapped her in. Thoughts of Daniel broke through, flooding her with guilt and regret. What was she doing?

She broke apart and pushed Evan away. "Stop! I can't do this."

Afterward, Chloe couldn't have said what made her glance over at Brianna in her high chair. A mother's instinct? Guilt, that her daughter should witness her mother betraying her father?

Except that when she did look, Brianna's eyes were glazed, her face was blue and her mouth wide open in some awful parody of laughter. While Chloe had been kissing Evan, Brianna had been choking on a piece of bread.

Chloe screamed.

Evan reacted instantly, his training overriding his aroused state to thrust Chloe aside and reach for Brianna. He dragged the baby from her high chair and scooped his finger into her mouth. Then turning her over with one hand under her solar plexus, he gave her a sharp rap between the shoulder blades. Nothing happened. "Call 911."

While Chloe grabbed for the wall phone, he repeated the thump between Brianna's shoulders, his mind leapfrogging ahead to the possibility of a tracheotomy. Pray God it wouldn't come to that. He repeated the maneuver a third time, and a chunk of half-eaten bread came shooting out of Brianna's mouth.

Instead of reviving, however, she lay limp and unresponsive in his arms. He lay her on the counter and loosened her clothes. A finger at her neck found a thin, erratic pulse, but her color was still cyanotic. How long had she been without oxygen while he and Chloe had kissed? Guilt played no part in his calculations; becoming emotional would only impair his ability to treat the child.

He bent to cover Brianna's mouth and nose with his own mouth and breathed lightly. Counting, one, two, three. Again, one, two, three. And again. *Come on, darlin'*. Yet even as he calmly proceeded to work at resuscitating her, his thoughts ran wild on a parallel track. Brianna could be his daughter. Why had he thrown away his chance with Chloe? If Brianna lived, he would change; he'd settle down. He would—

Brianna coughed. Her small lungs heaved and shuddered. Her skin began to turn pink. Evan's vision blurred. Thank God. Thank God.

Gathering up the child, he held her to his chest for

a moment, feeling her heart race as she hiccuped and sobbed, then let loose a huge wail that had Chloe reaching for her, clutching her and swaying as she tried to soothe her. "It's okay, sweetheart. You're okay." She glanced at Evan. "Should I cancel the ambulance?"

"Yes, but we'll still take her to the hospital."

"Why?" Chloe asked. "She's breathing. She's fine."

"We don't know how long she was choking, and even after the obstruction was removed she was unresponsive." Evan held a finger in front of Brianna's eyes and slowly moved it from side to side. She followed in one direction, then stopped watching. "You need to have her assessed."

"Do you mean for brain damage?" Chloe asked, horrified.

He could see her thoughts. A moment's indiscretion might mean a lifetime handicap for Chloe's daughter. "It takes six minutes before oxygen deprivation causes brain damage. I think she's fine, but we need to make certain. Let's go. The sooner, the better."

"Neither of us can drive. We've been drinking," Chloe said, shame twisting her features.

"It takes a lot more than that to make me drunk these days," Evan said dryly. Alcohol had become something of a problem for him; one he was doing his best to ignore.

"I can't leave this mess. Daniel will know you were

here." She looked around at the bottles and glasses, the dirty plates and scraps of food—evidence of an afternoon of debauchery. Her shoulders sagged. "I'll have to tell him, anyway. Especially if Brianna is…" Her eyes welled with tears and she shook her head. "Oh, God."

"Listen to me." Evan took her by the shoulders. "Brianna choked on a piece of bread, when you weren't looking. No one watches a fourteen-month-old baby constantly. It could have happened anytime—while you were stirring a pot on the stove or while you were making a sandwich."

"But it didn't! It happened when we were—"

He gave her a little shake. "Chloe, I'm telling you this for your sake. For Daniel's sake. You do not have to tell him you were kissing me. Understand? It would only make things worse."

Part of him wondered why he was giving her this advice. If Daniel divorced Chloe, he could have her. He'd come here not just to see his brother but also to see *her*. To find out if he was still attracted, if he was in love, how much he wanted her. A lot, obviously. But was it enough to disrupt all their lives? Enough to marry her? He thought he'd settled the matter once, and then he'd found he couldn't stay away. He still wasn't ready to give up his freedom, but what he hadn't counted on was his gut reaction to Brianna. If she *was* his daughter, how could he just leave without fighting for her?

He got Chloe and Brianna into his rental car and headed out on the narrow coastal road leading into the city. Chloe called Daniel on her cell phone, her fingers pleating the fabric of her skirt.

"Brianna's *fine,* I'm sure she's fine," Chloe kept saying. "We're just getting her checked…" She broke off, eyes scrunching shut as she realized what she'd let slip. After a pause, she added, "Evan. He's in town to see his brother." There was a longer pause. "He *saved* her. Okay, I'll see you there. Hurry." She hung up and turned to Evan. "You'll stay, won't you, until Daniel gets there?"

"Of course," Evan said, gripping the steering wheel. Despite the way Chloe had responded to his kiss, she seemed to feel something more than loyalty to her husband. Could she actually love the man? Would she still feel that way if he proved not to be Brianna's father? Would she stay with Daniel if Evan asked her to leave with him?

A triage nurse saw them right away and it wasn't long before an E.R. doctor called them into the examining room. Evan explained the situation to Dr. Sarah Rush, whose calm gray eyes flicked back and forth between him and Chloe. Chloe clutched a whimpering Brianna in her arms and bit her lip, trying not to cry.

"Have a seat and let's take a look," Dr. Rush said, wasting no time. With Brianna sitting in Chloe's lap, the doctor took the baby's pulse and blood pressure, then pulled out a penlight and examined the child's pupils. "How long was she unconscious?"

"I…I don't know," Chloe said. "I wasn't paying attention. We…I was busy with something else." Each word was pulled from her as if it were a painful extraction.

"I estimate between two and four minutes," Evan said, squeezing Chloe's hand. *Had* it been only a couple minutes? How long was a kiss? He'd lost track of time completely. In fact, for those few minutes he'd forgotten Brianna's existence entirely.

Chloe kept glancing between her watch and the door. "Daniel will be here soon. He won't know where to find us. That's my husband," she added to the doctor.

The doctor glanced from Chloe to Evan. "You're not the baby's father?"

A heart beat went by. With Chloe's hand gripped tightly in his, Evan answered, "No."

The doctor's pager beeped. She slung her stethoscope around her neck and checked the message. "Excuse me, I'll just be a few minutes," she said to Chloe and Evan and left the room.

Chloe glanced at her watch again. "I'm going to see if Daniel's in the waiting room. Will you stay with Brianna?" He nodded and she handed Brianna to him. Then she, too, hurried out.

Brianna settled naturally into the crook of Evan's arm and gave him a solemn trusting look that tugged at his heart, eliciting an unexpected feeling of tenderness. If she *was* his baby, was he right to leave her to another man to raise? To hell with what was right or wrong, the plain fact was that if she was his he wanted to know.

It occurred to him then that he was alone with the child in a hospital and had access to vials and swabs. He might never have another opportunity like this. Keeping an eye on both doors to the examining room, he started pulling open drawers, scrabbling through cotton pads, antiseptic wipes, surgical instruments... Aha, vials. He popped the cap off an empty clean vial and picked up a wooden tongue depressor.

"Open your mouth, sweetheart. That's it... Just a little more." How soft her skin was, like a rose petal. Plump and round and pink, so unlike the emaciated African children he'd been treating. "You're a lucky little girl," he murmured, gently scraping the inside of her cheek.

Brianna's blue eyes darkened in surprise and betrayal and her bottom lip began to wobble. Evan broke the wooden depressor in half so it would fit inside the container. He screwed on the lid and pocketed the vial. Then he whirled Brianna around in his arms and turned her tears into giggles.

"Sorry about that," Dr. Rush said, coming back into the room. She smiled when she saw Evan playing with the child. "This little one certainly seems to be all right, but let's finish checking her out. Now, where were we?"

Chloe returned with Daniel just as the doctor put down her instruments. Daniel ignored Evan and went straight to Brianna, his gaze searching her for evidence of harm. What did Daniel think he would find, Evan wondered—that she'd suddenly grown two heads?

"Brianna appears to be fine," Dr. Rush assured them. "Check in with your GP in a week. Sooner, if Brianna exhibits any abnormal behavior."

"What kind of behavior?" Chloe asked anxiously.

"Unusual irritability, lack of coordination. Those things can be difficult to diagnose in a toddler," the physician explained. "Just keep an eye on her."

"We'll watch her like a hawk," Daniel assured her.

Evan trailed behind Chloe and Daniel as they exited the hospital. He was under no illusion that he'd be invited back to the house, but he couldn't leave without saying goodbye to Chloe. Once in the parking lot Daniel planted himself as a solid barrier between the two, however. Now that the crisis was over, all semblance of cooperation between the two men vanished.

Daniel was still in his work clothes—scuffed boots, plaid shirt and faded blue jeans. Bits of sawdust were caught in his thick, dark hair and his black eyebrows pulled together in a scowl. "I suppose you think I should thank you for saving my child."

Evan couldn't help taunt him. "How do you know she's yours?"

A deep flush came over Daniel's tanned face, turning it brick red. "I don't know what you're doing here," he growled, "but stay the hell away from my wife and daughter."

Evan rolled his eyes. "You're as predictable as the backwoods you've buried Chloe in. As it happens, I'm going back to Australia so you can put your mind at ease. Just don't take her for granted, or you'll lose her."

"Don't tell me how to treat my wife," Daniel warned. His clenched fist came up, threatening Evan. "For two cents I'd beat the crap out of you right now."

"Your wife," Evan mocked with a disdain that was pure bluff. Daniel had four inches and thirty pounds on him and could no doubt flatten him. But Evan's parting shot was calculated to deliver a blow more deadly than any physical punch or jab. "Just remember that *I* had her first."

Chapter 5

The bubbles had moved so far offshore that Chloe could no longer distinguish them from the foam that flecked the crests of the waves. She huddled inside her duffel coat and jammed gloved fingers into her armpits, seeking warmth. Daniel had come out of the garage suddenly this morning. Had he seen Evan kissing her?

Brianna approached, holding something in one closed fist as she leaped lightly from rock to rock. Her eyes were bright with excitement and her golden hair curled in the moist air. Nowadays she studied marine biology at university, but Chloe was reminded of the way she'd been as a child, running to show off her treasures from the sea.

"Look what I found." Brianna unfurled her fingers

to reveal a green crab with a spiky shell and long, thin legs. "It's a kelp crab."

"That's...fascinating." Chloe hoped she'd mustered sufficient enthusiasm.

"Never mind," Brianna said, laughing. "I know this is about as interesting to you as slime mold." She returned the crab to the kelp forest that swayed against the rocks with every wave and sat down beside her mother. "They must be nearly at the wreck by now. I wish I didn't have this cold so I could have gone, too," she added for the twentieth time that morning.

"I hope your father is okay." No sooner had Chloe spoken than she felt Brianna grow tense. Feeling her daughter's gaze on her, she turned. "What is it?"

"Which one of them is my father, just out of interest's sake?" Brianna asked matter-of-factly, her bright blue eyes fixed on Chloe.

Chloe was as shocked by Brianna's practical tone as she was by the question itself. Her daughter might resemble her, but now and then she came out with statements that made Chloe realize how different they were in personality. Whose daughter was she, indeed?

"Wh-what makes you ask a thing like that?" she stammered. "Daniel is your father, of course."

"Mom, I know you had a love affair with Evan just before you met Dad and that I was born six months after you were married. It's a natural question." She put her arm around Chloe. "I would never renounce Dad or anything like that. I'd just like to know for sure."

"How did you know about me and Evan?"

"Evan told me while he was suiting up. He said you were the love of his life."

"He had no business telling you that," Chloe said angrily. *How could she describe the complicated emotional circumstances that had led her to give up the man she loved in order to marry another man who was prepared to take care of her daughter? Then she realized Brianna wasn't asking for those sorts of explanations. All she wanted to know about was the matter of her paternity.* *"I don't know,"* Chloe said finally. *"We never had a DNA test. Maybe it's time we did."*

Brianna turned her gaze out to sea. "I wonder."

"What do you wonder?"

"Just the way Evan looked at me this morning… I think he already knows."

"The plant nursery is delivering the topsoil and shrubs first thing this morning." Chloe poured Daniel another cup of coffee and went to the kitchen window to peer out at the overcast sky. The sun was just breaking through the clouds, gilding the yellowing leaves on the birch trees across the road. "Looks as though it'll stay fine long enough for us to get the dirt spread and the plants in the ground." She turned back to Daniel. "Do you want more pancakes or bacon?"

"No, thanks. Breakfast was delicious, but I'm about to burst." Daniel pushed his chair back from the table and stretched his legs. "With all this cooking you've been doing lately, I'll have to start watching what I eat."

"Sorry," she said automatically. "I just wanted to—" She broke off, flushing, unable to finish the sentence. *She wanted to make up for kissing Evan.*

Daniel knew she felt guilty about Brianna, but Chloe couldn't tell him about the kiss. A month had gone by, and she still felt awful about what had happened. *Sorry, sorry, sorry.* The refrain ran through her head all day, every day.

Daniel's shrewd glance over his coffee cup made her turn to wipe Brianna's syrup-smeared chin. "More milk, honey?"

Brianna shook her head, happily squishing a piece of soggy pancake into her mouth.

Chloe wished she could erase from her memory the whole horrible episode. If she'd been inattentive a minute or two longer, their precious little girl might be brain damaged or dead. Her marriage would have disintegrated the moment Daniel had found out why. How could she have forgotten for even a second that she was a mother and a wife?

"Stop fussing, Chloe, and eat your own breakfast," Daniel told her. "What are we going to do with Miss Muffin while we're shoveling topsoil?"

"Your mom's coming over to look after her." Chloe forced herself to sit down and take pancakes from the platter. After a couple of bites, however, she put down her fork and got up to clear the table. With her stomach constantly in a knot, she'd lost her taste for food.

Daniel wrapped an arm around her hips as she passed and pulled her onto his lap. His hands slid up her rib cage, his fingers probing each bony bump and hollow. "You'll waste away to nothing if you don't eat more. I can feel every rib."

"I'm fine." She slid her fingers into his hair, sifting through the silky black waves, but she couldn't quite bring herself to meet his gaze. Her hands dropped to her lap.

"If you're so fine, then why this sudden frenzy around the house? The cooking, the landscaping, the decorating…" He gestured with his head to the living room, where books of fabric swatches were stacked next to their old couch. "Not that I object to anything you're doing, but you've gone crazy with it."

"I'm just keeping busy." Chloe said, stifling a yawn.

"You don't sleep," he continued. "You're up half the night when Brianna's teething, then you drag yourself out of bed at five a.m. to make me breakfast. It's sweet, but I don't need you to do that."

"I want to take care of my family," she said, fiddling nervously with a button on his shirt. "What's wrong with that?"

"Nothing—as long as you take care of yourself, too." Daniel paused. "I think you're feeling guilty about what happened." She glanced up at him, alarmed. "Brianna is *okay*." At the mention of her daughter's name, Chloe glanced over her shoulder to make sure she really was all right. Daniel gently pulled Chloe's face back to him. "Stop beating yourself up. You're a nervous wreck. It was a terrible accident—but it wasn't your fault."

Chloe dropped her head, letting her hair fall over her face. An awful silence settled over the kitchen.

Daniel pushed a long curl behind his wife's ear and tilted her chin, forcing her to meet his gaze. "Chloe, is there something you're not telling me?"

The love and concern in his dark brown eyes broke her down. "I...I feel badly because I was distracted by Evan when it happened."

A muscle twitched in Daniel's jaw. "You two had quite the party."

"We got *drunk*." Chloe thumped Daniel's chest lightly with a splayed hand, angry at herself and frustrated with him. "Aren't you mad at me? Not just because I was so irresponsible about Brianna, but because I was with *him?*"

Daniel's jaw clenched tighter and Chloe felt the muscles in his chest stiffen. "How do you mean, *with* him?"

Her startled gaze shot to his as she realized he'd misunderstood. "Not *that*."

"Mama! Me want down," Brianna demanded, banging a sticky hand on the high-chair tray.

Chloe slid off Daniel's lap and rinsed a cloth under

the tap to wipe the toddler's hands and face. Then she took off the soiled bib and lifted Brianna onto the floor. Brianna ran out to the living room where her toys were heaped on an activity mat.

The bib still crumpled in her hand, Chloe watched the small child from the doorway. She heard the scrape of Daniel's chair as he rose and came to stand behind her, close enough to make her skin prickle.

"What happened, Chloe?" There was no gentleness in his voice now, only a calm demand for the truth.

Chloe's chest squeezed tight. "He…kissed me."

The silence hummed with tension.

"What did *you* do?"

"I k-kissed him back."

"And that's what you were doing while Brianna choked." His voice had gone dead and flat.

A sob pushed up from her lungs and caught in her throat. "Daniel, I'm so sorry."

Chloe hugged herself as tears ran down her cheeks. She ached for Daniel's arms to close around her in forgiveness, but that wasn't going to happen. She almost wished that he would shout, break things. Give way to a violent emotional storm that would batter but ultimately cleanse their relationship. His controlled withdrawal from her scared her more than fury. She heard his footsteps moving away from her across the tiled floor and a moment later the door to the garage shut quietly but decisively.

"Mama," Brianna trotted over, lifting her arms. "Mama, *up.*"

Chloe lifted Brianna into her arms. More tears fell into the little one's hair as she hugged her daughter close. Then she wiped her eyes with the back of a hand and squared her shoulders. She didn't have time for pity, nor did she deserve it.

"Let's get you dressed," she said, forcing a wobbly note of cheer into her voice as she carried Brianna down the hall to her bedroom. "Grandma's coming soon."

Chloe was pulling a bright blue sweater over Brianna's golden head when she heard the front door open and Daniel's mother, Lynn, call out, "Hello! Anybody home?"

Brianna squirmed out of Chloe's grip and ran down the hall. "Gammy!"

Lynn's frosted blond hair brushed the shoulders of the hand-knit cardigan she wore over blue jeans as she bent to scoop Brianna into her arms. "How's my sweetheart?"

"Thanks for coming," Chloe said, kissing her mother-in-law's cheek.

"No problem." The older woman handed Chloe a bag of apples. "These are from the tree in our backyard." Then she drew back to study Chloe's face, her keen blue gaze taking in Chloe's red-rimmed eyes. "Are you all right?"

"I'm fine." Chloe smiled brightly. "If you don't

mind I'm going straight outside. Daniel and I want to get going on the landscaping, in case it rains later. Help yourself to coffee."

"Don't let Daniel work you too hard," Mrs. Bennett said. "You're looking very thin."

"Daniel takes good care of me. I'm *fine*, honestly." Chloe went out through the garage, slipping her feet into gum boots and picking up a pair of work gloves from the bench Daniel had built along the back wall.

Chloe could never tell Lynn why she'd been crying. Daniel had protected her image by not informing his parents that Evan was at the house when Brianna had choked. The least Chloe could do was maintain the fiction that Daniel had a wife he could be proud of. Especially since she wanted so badly for him to *be* proud of her.

Just as she came outside a dump truck was backing into the driveway and Daniel was directing the driver to deposit his load of topsoil in the front yard. The truck's box lifted and the metal gate on the back clanged open, spilling four tons of rich black soil onto the ground. No sooner had the dump truck left than a flatbed truck arrived, bringing two dozen cedar trees for a hedge and a liquid amber sapling, already blazing red and gold, that Chloe had chosen for the front yard.

Daniel got busy spreading the topsoil with a Bobcat and Chloe followed him, raking the soil smooth. He barely glanced at her as he jolted forward and back, scraping and pushing at the dirt. The roar of the diesel engine made conversation impossible. Chloe was just as glad, welcoming the break from thinking, feeling, worrying. Now that she'd told him the truth, she felt better. She would make amends, but there was hard work ahead.

Three hours later, Daniel was digging holes for the cedar trees and Chloe was evening off the last corner of the yard. She leaned on her rake and pushed the damp straggling hair off her forehead. Time for a break.

A scrap of bright blue caught her eye and she spotted Brianna emerging from the house and making her way across the clods of dirt, brandishing a plastic rake. Too cute. Chloe was about to call to Daniel to look when Brianna turned and Chloe's smile vanished abruptly.

Brianna's cheeks bulged like a squirrel with a horde of nuts. Chloe reacted instinctively, her brain instantly seeing Brianna's face tinged with blue. Throwing down her rake Chloe raced across the yard, her boots sinking craters in the soft loam. *"Brianna!"*

"What's the matter?" Daniel called, looking up from the hole he was digging.

"She's got something in her mouth!"

Daniel threw down his shovel, his long strides eating up the ground as he raced over.

Chloe dropped to her knees in the dirt in front of Brianna. "Spit it out. *Spit it out.*"

Brianna shook her head, glowering at Chloe, and

she jammed a fist in her mouth. Immediately she gagged and her eyes rolled back in her head.

Chloe tugged Brianna's hand away from her face. Daniel snatched Brianna up and turned her upside down over his arm. He was about to rap her between the shoulder blades when Brianna coughed. A blob of melting ice cream fell out of her mouth and plopped onto a mound of dirt, rolling down the sides like icy pink volcanic lava.

Chloe's gasp turned to a laughing sob as she collapsed in the dirt, her heart still pounding. "Oh, my God! I thought…"

She didn't bother finishing. They'd both thought the same thing. Daniel shifted Brianna upright and settled her in the crook of one arm. Then he peeled off a glove and wiped the ice cream off her chin with a blunt dirt-smeared thumb.

Chloe struggled to her feet, with Daniel reaching down to help her. She clung to his hand, seeking his gaze, but his eyes flicked away and reluctantly she let go. A painful hollow formed in her chest as she realized how much she'd taken his touch for granted.

"Brianna, there you are, you little monkey!" Lynn came running out of the house. "I was just getting my shoes on when she went flying out," she explained to Chloe and Daniel. "Come on, sweetheart," she cooed, taking her from Daniel's arms. "Let's go down to the beach and let Mommy and Daddy work."

"Beach!" Brianna shouted excitedly. Daniel's mother bore the little girl away around the side of the house.

Daniel picked up his glove off the ground and slapped it clean against a pant leg. "We can't have a heart attack every time she puts something in her mouth."

"I know, but if you'd seen her that day. I've never been so frightened." Even now Chloe felt a pain in her stomach just thinking about it.

His mouth twisted. "I can imagine. Still, we have to get over it."

"Can *you*?" she asked quietly. She wasn't just talking about Brianna choking.

Daniel's jaw set and he turned away, heading back to the spot where he was digging. Chloe followed. Having begun, she needed to continue their talk, needed some kind of reassurance that Daniel was going to forgive her. "Daniel, please listen to me. Yes, Evan kissed me, but then I pushed him away. I know who I'm married to. Whether you believe me or not, my vows mean something to me."

Daniel picked up his shovel and stabbed it into the ground, slicing a thick wedge of dirt off the side of the hole. "Time will tell."

"But, Daniel…"

He leaned on his shovel, his face settling into weary grooves. "Let it go, Chloe. Just let it go."

Dissatisfied but not blaming Daniel, Chloe had

no choice but to go back to work. At noon, Lynn brought out sandwiches and a thermos of lemonade. Chloe sat on the front steps next to Daniel, her cast-off gloves lying palm up on the concrete like pleading hands. They ate quickly and without talking. Chloe nibbled on a ham-and-cheese sandwich, her stomach churning even though she was famished. Her arms and shoulders ached and blisters were forming on her palms and the inside of one thumb. If this could serve as penance, she'd surely have atoned for some of her failings by now.

The sun was a red streak over the ocean and the shadows were gathering in the pines when they finally threw the last shovelful of dirt around the liquid amber and tamped it down. Chloe went around the yard gathering up shovels and rakes while Daniel drove the rented Bobcat up the ramp onto his pickup truck, ready to return in the morning.

Chloe walked into the middle of the deserted road and looked back at all they'd accomplished. The warm sienna timber of the ranch-style house glowed in the setting sun and the fresh topsoil was black and smooth, ready for seeding. An even row of young cedars marked the front edge of the yard and ran down the side of the property opposite the driveway. In the center stood the liquid amber, radiant in red and gold, fluttering its leaves in the onshore breeze.

Daniel padlocked the chain around the Bobcat, anchoring it to the truck, and came to stand next to her.

Together they gazed at their accomplishments in silence, then his arm stole around her waist and he drew her to his side.

Chloe felt her eyes fill, but she didn't dare look up at him for fear of bursting into tears. She slipped an arm around Daniel's hips and treasured his solid warmth in the rapidly chilling evening air. Then she felt his fingers brush her temple as he pushed back her hair to press his lips where her heart beat close beneath the surface.

"We make a good team," he whispered huskily.

"We do at that." A tear slipped free from her lashes and slid down her cheek to be caught in the crease of her smile. "I think I'll sleep well tonight."

Chapter 6

The shipwreck loomed ahead, an elongated mass lying with its starboard side embedded in the ocean floor. As Daniel and Evan approached, indistinct shapes resolved themselves into the curve of the bow and the jutting angle of the wheelhouse. The remnants of a funnel lay ten yards away, half buried in sediment. The rusted metal hull was pockmarked with gaping holes and heavily encrusted with coralline algae and bryozoans.

For Daniel, the reality of where he was and what he was doing suddenly sunk in. He was about to explore the ruined hulk of a steamship that had plied the coastal waters between Seattle and Alaska more than a hundred years ago. It was a piece of history, broken on the rocky coastline that was known as the Graveyard of the Pacific.

His fears and anxiety over the dive, his outrage over Evan's treachery, all faded as he reached out and touched the hull. When Evan had turned up at the dive meeting with his brother, Daniel had been filled with rage knowing Chloe's old boyfriend was back in town. But if Evan hadn't agreed to be his buddy, Daniel might not have been able to participate. He turned to Evan and gave him a big thumbs-up.

"Hurry, sweetheart, or we're going to be late for your first day of school." Chloe watched five-year-old Brianna fumble with her laces, determined to tie the bow on her new shoes herself. The blue ribbons on the ends of Brianna's braids quivered with the effort of concentration.

Chloe glanced at her watch and curled her fingers into her palms to stop herself from taking over and getting the job done. She heard Daniel's truck pull into the driveway and glanced up in surprise. He'd left for work two hours ago. What was he doing home?

"I did it, Mommy!" Brianna proclaimed triumphantly.

"Wonderful. Quickly, now, let's get going." Chloe grabbed Brianna's school bag and took her daughter by the hand. They went out the door to see Daniel coming up the steps two at a time. His dark hair was mussed and his blue workpants were dusty with plaster.

Daniel tugged on one of Brianna's braids. "All ready for school?"

"Are you coming, too, Daddy?" Brianna asked, bouncing down the steps.

"I wouldn't miss it." Daniel turned to Chloe. "Have you got the camera?"

"In my purse." She gave him a warm smile and kissed his cheek, tasting salty sweat and grit. "What a wonderful surprise. You didn't tell me you were planning on coming."

"I wasn't sure I could get away." He hustled them down the steps and opened the rear door to Chloe's battered blue Volvo so Brianna could climb in.

Chloe got in the driver's seat and started the car. It was practically an antique, but Daniel had insisted on buying it because it was safe.

Daniel helped Brianna put on her seat belt. Then he tickled her under the chin. "All set?"

Brianna giggled. "You bet!"

While Chloe drove the narrow coastal road into Sooke, Daniel leaned over the back of his seat and teased Brianna. The little girl tossed him cheeky replies. Chloe smiled, listening to them, and occasionally glanced in the rear-view mirror at her daughter or sideways at her husband. Brianna's strawberries-and-cream coloring might look nothing like Daniel's olive skin and near-black hair, but they were quite the pair of jokers. Brianna's eyes were a brighter blue than Chloe's indigo color, although her determined little chin was surely a chip off Daniel's strong jaw.

Oh, what did it matter? Chloe asked herself impatiently for the millionth time as she found herself wondering whether Daniel or Evan had fathered her child. Daniel was the man who'd helped her into this world, the man who was taking her to school… He was her father, regardless of whose DNA she possessed.

"Chloe?" Daniel's voice broke into her thoughts. "Wasn't that the turnoff to the school back there?"

"Oh, shoot!" Chloe slowed abruptly, then sped up again as the car behind her came right up to her bumper. She put on her turn indicator and pulled into the first side street she came to, laboriously making a three-point turn in someone's driveway before getting back onto the right road. "There's a parking spot. I'd better grab it. With all the parents coming to see their children off, this place will be a zoo today."

They joined the throng of excited children and moms and dads funneling up the concrete pathway to the double front doors of the school. It was a warm sunny day, more like summer than fall though the air held the indefinable scent of changing seasons. Chloe led the way to Brianna's classroom, which they'd visited the previous June in order to meet Brianna's teacher and familiarize her with the school.

Miss Petoe, an attractive young brunette with a big smile, stood in the doorway welcoming her new pupils. Amazingly, she greeted them all—including Brianna—by name.

"How does she do that?" Daniel whispered in Chloe's ear as they hovered outside in the hall.

"She took photos of everyone when they visited in the spring," Chloe whispered back. "She must have been up all night memorizing names and faces. Look, Brianna's so eager to start school she's forgotten all about us."

But when Brianna was halfway into the classroom she suddenly realized her parents weren't with her. She spun around and ran back to cling to Chloe's pant legs, her eyes wide and her lower lip trembling.

"You're going to have a wonderful time here, sweetheart," Chloe said, smoothing her daughter's wispy bangs away from her forehead. "We'll be back to pick you up when school's over."

"I'll show you to your desk." Miss Petoe gently took Brianna's hand and led her away, talking to distract her.

Daniel chuckled. "She looks as though she's marching to her doom, but she's determined to be brave."

Chloe choked out a laugh as she felt Daniel's arm go around her shoulder in a comforting squeeze. She exchanged a proud glance with him before taking a last lingering look at their little girl.

Miss Petoe started to close the door.

"Quick, did you get a picture?" Daniel asked Chloe.

Chloe dug through her purse for her camera and edged into the doorway. "Brianna!"

Brianna, sitting up very straight in her new desk,

turned her head and smiled. Chloe clicked and captured the moment.

She didn't break down until she tried to unlock the Volvo, fumbling when she couldn't see where to put the key. With a sob she fell into Daniel's arms and as she felt them tighten around her she was grateful for his quiet strength. "Oh, my goodness," she gasped. "I never thought I'd be so emotional."

"Never mind. It's okay," he said softly in her ear as he stroked her spine with his strong hand. "Just think of all the free time you'll have." When her only reply was a deep sigh, he added, "Will you be all right? I hate to go back to work and leave you alone."

"I'll be fine," she sniffed, pulling herself together. "I'll just have to take more ballet students to keep busy. I've been thinking about starting a preschool class."

"That's a good idea." Daniel looked up at the clear blue sky. "You know, we're not going to get many more of these beautiful days before the wet weather sets in. I'll call Rob and tell him I'm not coming back. We'll go for a picnic."

Chloe brightened. "Can you afford the time off?"

"Yeah, sure. I can't do a whole lot more on the house we're working on until the plasterer is finished anyway." He kissed the moisture away from her eyes. "What do you say? A loaf of bread, a jug of wine and thou—on the beach?"

"Always the beach," she groaned, breaking into laughter. "We live on the damn beach."

"I like the beach. Don't you like it?" He bent down to kiss her, a warm, wet openmouthed kiss that set her heart to fluttering. "We don't often get time to ourselves in the middle of the day. Let's take advantage of it."

They stopped at the deli, the bakery and finally the liquor store, where Daniel picked out an expensive bottle of wine. Chloe was about to comment on his extravagance when he gave her a warm, sexy smile that was positively indecent at ten o'clock on a weekday morning in a suburban shopping center.

Anticipation buzzed through her. She stopped thinking about all the things she ought to be doing, like laundry and cleaning the bathroom, and started looking forward to spending the day alone with Daniel.

"This is fun," she said as they hurried back to the car with their bags of goodies. "It's been ages since we've done anything spontaneous."

They drove to Mystic Beach, a long stretch of deserted sand where whitecapped swells rolled in to crash on the shore. Daniel put the blanket and cooler down next to a log and they walked to the edge of the water. The sky was a brilliant blue, the air unusually still and the sun unseasonably warm, even for early September.

"Let's go swimming," Daniel suggested, and without waiting for her reply, pulled his shirt over his head.

"Are you kidding?" she demanded. "We'll freeze!"

"Don't be a sissy." Matter-of-factly, he dropped

his pants on the sand. Then his boxers. His tanned torso and thighs contrasted strongly with the whiteness of his hips.

Scandalized, Chloe glanced around. "Skinny-dipping in public?"

"You're supposed to be the uninhibited one," he teased. "Anyway, there's no one around for miles."

Chloe scanned the dark fir trees and the fringe of glossy green salal bushes that came down to the rocky shore. If anyone bushwhacked his way through that, he deserved an eyeful. What the heck? She kicked off her sandals and rapidly shed her T-shirt and slacks.

That's when she realized there *was* someone around—Daniel. And he was getting an eyeful. Although they'd been married five years and had seen each other in various states of undress many times, standing naked on a beach in broad daylight like some modern day Adam and Eve was different. She felt his gaze drift over her body from her breasts down to the thatch of auburn between her legs. Her blood quickened with excitement, seeing him aroused, and instinctively she moved toward him.

His skin was hot where it touched her breasts, her belly, the tops of her thighs. A light breeze played over her back, lifting her hair. His hands held her clenched buttocks when she overbalanced in the soft sand and he pulled her hard against him. An ache developed low in her groin.

He kissed her, his tongue dipping briefly inside her

mouth before withdrawing. "Are we going in the water or what?"

She pressed her hands against his chest, pushing him away. "Last one in is a rotten egg." Squealing like a teenager, she splashed into the shallows, stopping with a gasp. "It *is* freezing!"

Daniel roared up behind her, scooped her into his arms and carried her out until the water was waist-deep, then dumped her, screaming, into the icy water. She came up gasping, the cold tingling her skin, the salt stinging her eyes. He was laughing at her, his teeth white against his tanned skin, beads of water glittering in his black hair. With a cry she pushed him backward off his feet. Then they were floating together, arms entwined, legs tangled, mouths fused. She hardly noticed the cold until a cresting wave splashed over her face and she came up, spluttering.

Daniel dove into the next wave, white foam crashing over his brown shoulders and sleek back. For over an hour they played in the sea, bodysurfing, floating on their backs, tumbling together through the water like otters. Finally they staggered onto the shore, exhausted and invigorated, wrapping themselves in thick towels and blinking the seawater from their eyelashes.

Chloe spread the blanket and Daniel opened the wine. They drank crisp, cool sauvignon blanc and ate ravenously of savory pastries, fresh-peeled prawns dipped straight into a jar of cocktail sauce and chunks of spicy sausage.

Chloe glanced at Daniel, with his towel draped low on his hips and his big muscular body relaxed, his dark hair tossed like stormy waves. He was good for her in so many ways, she thought. He was fun to do things with, they conversed easily about almost anything, and best of all she could be herself. Plus, she felt safe with him. Not just financially secure—although she knew he made sure they lived within their means—but safe, knowing that his love was constant and unconditional. No matter what happened, he would be there for her. And the sex was good, since she'd gotten over feeling as though she was betraying Evan. Years ago now.

In fact, the sex was great. Her and Daniel's relationship had evolved to the point where she truly felt Daniel was not just a friend but also her husband and lover.

So why could she not stop thinking about Evan? Would some small part of her always wonder "what if?" If she hadn't married Daniel, if she'd waited for Evan, would they be as happy as she and Daniel were? Would they be happier?

"You're very quiet," Daniel said.

Chloe drained the last of her wine and smiled. "Just enjoying the peace. It's a perfect day."

Perfect until her thoughts had turned to Evan. She wasn't ever completely honest about him because she didn't want to hurt Daniel. But this endless speculation was pointless; she had to stop.

Thoughtfully, Daniel took the wine bottle out of the cooler and refilled their glasses. "Have you heard from Evan since that time Brianna choked—what was it, four years ago?"

Four years and three months. God, he'd done it again, picked up on her thoughts. She was surprised he'd broached the subject—he never had before. It was as if Daniel hoped that by not talking about Evan he wouldn't exist.

"I thought you would have known," she tried to say lightly, although the tension in her voice was apparent. "You always seemed to be aware when a letter came."

His salt-encrusted lashes narrowed against the sun. "I never knew what he wrote in them."

She destroyed the letters after she'd memorized them, but she'd always wondered if Daniel had found and read them, too. It was a relief to know he'd respected her privacy. At what cost to his own peace of mind? Not knowing, he must have imagined the worst.

"He wrote once more, not long after he got back to Australia," she said. "He was working in an Aboriginal community in the outback. He said he still loved me. He…" She broke off to catch her breath. This was painful to both of them, but she owed Daniel an explanation. "He asked me to leave you and come to him. He wanted Brianna, too."

Daniel's mouth clamped tight. "What did you say?"

"I'm still here, aren't I?"

"You must have known I wouldn't let Brianna

go," Daniel said. "And I can't imagine you leaving her behind."

"No, I would never do that," Chloe conceded. She held his gaze. "But my decision to stay wasn't just because of Brianna. I made a vow to you and I intend to keep it."

Daniel nodded, and his shoulders seemed to relax. "And that's the end of it?"

"I wrote Evan back and told him I wasn't coming. I asked him not to write to me again. He hasn't."

Daniel nodded, satisfied. Then he got to his feet, dropping the towel. "Let's walk down the beach."

"Stark naked?" Chloe's eyes roamed up his body to meet his amused gaze.

He grinned. "Why not?"

They walked hand in hand, leaving footprints on the wet sand, and talked about Chloe's ballet classes, about the possibility of her going back to dancing now that Brianna was in school—not as a soloist, of course, but in the *corps de ballet*. Chloe also wanted to take some university courses. Daniel supported all her ambitions. His business was growing, and they could afford child care when Chloe needed to be at a performance.

Something had changed between them, Chloe thought. There was a lightness that hadn't been there before, an openness. Now that she and Daniel had finally talked about Evan, maybe she would stop thinking about the other man. What if it had been that simple all along, just being totally honest with Daniel?

Stretching her arms to the sky, she pirouetted across the sand, leaping and dipping to the music in her head. In spite of all the good things about their marriage, she'd always felt slightly constrained when she danced around Daniel. Now the last of her reserve evaporated under the sun and beside the sea, leaving her lighter than air, dancing for the seagulls and the watching trees. Dancing for herself, for Daniel, for the pure joy of moving.

Daniel smiled in admiration, then drifted off on his own to wander up to the flat black rocks on the point. When she eventually caught up with him again he was flat on his stomach, peering into a tide pool. Purple and red anemones squatted fatly among waving green algae, orange starfish were plastered to the rocky sides of the pool and hermit crabs scuttled over the bottom, dragging their snail shells.

"Amazing, isn't it?" he said. "It's like a little town down there with all the different inhabitants."

"You should have been a marine biologist," she said.

"I don't know about that," he said. "I never liked school much. Always preferred working with my hands."

"What about taking up scuba diving?" she suggested. He was silent. "Daniel?"

"I tried once," he said flatly. "Couldn't do it."

"But you're a strong swimmer."

"I got claustrophobic," he explained. "Trussed up in a wet suit with all that gear on, a tank and weight belt, then the weight of the water pressing down on me... I couldn't breathe." His voice became tight just talking about it. "I'd give anything to be a diver. I know there's so much more to see down there..." Abruptly he rose and held out his hand to pull her up. "Let's go back to the blanket."

They walked back to their picnic spot. The sun and the wine and the exercise had combined to leave Chloe in a pleasantly tipsy state of drowsiness. She stretched out on her stomach on the blanket. "I think I'll have a snooze."

"That's not a bad idea." Daniel lay down beside her and she curled into the crook of his arm, her leg resting comfortably next to his.

When she awoke some time later, it was to feel him rubbing sunscreen over her back. "The sun's not strong enough to burn this time of year," she murmured.

He moved his hand lower, over her buttock and down the back of her leg. "Maybe I just like to touch you."

Blinking sleepily, she peered at him over her shoulder. "Be my guest."

Beneath his firm, warm strokes, she slowly awoke. His calloused fingertips on the insides of her thighs built a slow heat deep inside her, a low throbbing between her legs. When he'd covered every inch of her back, she rolled over so he could do her front.

He poured warmed lotion into the palm of his

hand, then smoothed it onto her chest below her collarbone. Then out of the blue he said, "I'd like us to have another baby."

They'd never discussed more children, mainly because their marriage so often seemed precarious, teetering as it did between genuine affection and Chloe's old love for Evan, gone but never entirely forgotten by either of them. Now the time seemed right. "I've been thinking about that, too," Chloe said. "Brianna needs a brother or sister and I...I'd like our next baby to be planned. An act of love."

Daniel's dark eyes lit. "A boy." Immediately, he retracted the thought. "Of course another girl would be great, too."

"It's okay. It's natural to want one of each," Chloe assured him with a laugh. Then silently she prayed she could give him a boy.

His loving gaze held hers as he rubbed in the lotion, stroking his way over her shoulders, her arms, her breasts, her midriff, lower and lower. She let him look his fill, enjoying the caress of both his eyes and his hand. He hardened and grew large and she wanted to take hold of him, but she made herself lie still, letting the tension build. She saw his eyes darken and felt her breath grow shallow, as if they were one, feeling everything the other felt. As his hand dipped between her legs, he leaned forward and covered her mouth with his. His tongue entered her at the same time his fingers slid inside.

Chloe reached for him then, arching against his hand, greedily matching him kiss for kiss. He removed his fingers and thrust inside her. The heat, the sun, the salt tang on his skin—her senses were saturated with something elemental and primitive. Welling up from deep inside came a feeling beyond affection, mutual goals and their shared love for Brianna. It was wonderful and unexpected and had grown quietly in the background over the years, as their lives became more closely intertwined.

"Daniel," she whispered. Her questing fingertips scraped the sharp angles of his jaw, traced the strong cords of his neck. "I love you."

He froze and she wondered what was wrong until she realized this was the first time she'd said those words and meant them in the way he'd always longed for. She felt ashamed, then, to think of the way she'd held back sometimes, when he'd given her so much love for so many years, never asking for any in return. She was about to ask his forgiveness when she felt a tremor start deep inside him, spreading outward as he began to move again. He rocked into her in powerful thrusts and then all thoughts vanished as the movement and pressure sent her over the edge. She came with the sun dazzling her eyes and the seagull's call in her ears and Daniel arching over her, lifting his face to the sun as a single tear slid down his sunburned cheek.

Chapter 7

What was that bastard saying to Chloe now? Daniel hoisted the weight belt over his hips and buckled it on, keeping one eye on Chloe and Evan who were talking in low tones not ten feet away as she double-checked his tank valve. He couldn't believe the nerve of the man, trying to seduce his wife right under his nose.

The memory of their overheard conversation that morning filled Daniel's chest like a fifty-pound lead weight, adding to the pressure from his tank and the constricting wet suit. He drew in a deep breath, trying to get oxygen into his lungs, but he felt squeezed flat, crushed by the mingling of Chloe's laughter with Evan's Aussie accent. Daniel was going to lose her to a goddamn Mick Dundee in neoprene.

Daniel awkwardly flapped backward over the cobbled beach in his fins, sweating with nerves and exertion. Getting into the cool water would be a relief—if only he didn't have to go under.

Chloe came running after him, her boots crunching on the wet stones, sliding on patches of kelp. "Hey, don't go without saying goodbye."

"Goodbye." He paused at the water's edge, an uneasy feeling in his gut. That sounded so final.

"Daniel?" Chloe's worried gaze searched his face. "Are you going to be all right? Don't forget your breathing. Imagine you're a cloud, remember."

She alone here, today, knew of Daniel's claustrophobia and how he'd learned to quell his anxiety by using positive visualization. Each dive involved a struggle between his desire to experience the undersea world and his panic at having thirty feet of water between him and the surface. Thirty feet? Hell, today they were going down to 110 feet. He broke out in a cold sweat just thinking about it.

"I'm fine, never better," he said.

"Stick with Evan. He'll look out for you."

"Evan—" Daniel began and broke off. This was no time to get involved in an argument. Instead, he took a couple quick breaths from his regulator to make sure it was working. Then he gave Chloe a long look, just in case it was their last. And he didn't mean because he was going to drown.

"Chloe, love, can you untangle my pressure gauge?" Evan said, walking over, fins in hand. He winked at Daniel and Daniel's fists clenched.

"Sure." Chloe reached over Evan's shoulder for the thin

rubber hose and the gauge that measured the amount of air left in his tank and threaded it through the tangle of straps. She got the pressure gauge free and exchanged a smile with Evan that made Daniel's blood boil.

"Thanks," Evan said, touching her on the arm. He turned to Daniel and stepped backward into the shallows, gliding easily as a merman. "Ready, mate?"

Daniel grunted and awkwardly heaved one foot after the other over the shifting stones. As his knees submerged, he gave up and fell into the water, then floundered to right himself, feeling like an ass. In front of Evan.

Still seething with anger, he moved into deeper water to clear his mask in preparation for a duck dive. When this dive was over, Evan would get what was coming to him.

"Uh, Daniel?" Chloe glanced at her watch over his bare shoulder as he labored over her. "I've got to be at class in an hour."

"For God's sake! Go then," he exclaimed and heaved himself off her. Nothing like a hurry up to kill the urge.

"I didn't mean for you to stop, just speed it up a little." She paused. "Honey?"

"I'm not a trained monkey," he grated, rolling onto his back. "I can't perform on demand. Forget it for now."

"But I'm ovulating! This could be the last day this cycle." She ran a hand down his belly onto his groin, trying to coax life back into him. "If we don't do it now, I won't be fertile for another month."

Daniel pushed her hand away and placed an arm over his eyes so he wouldn't see the mixture of hurt and frustration in hers. "Maybe if we stop trying so hard, something will happen."

"We've been trying for two years," she said. "Brianna is seven. Even if I got pregnant right now, there would be a huge age gap between them."

"Maybe if you didn't work all the time," he complained. "You're taking classes at the university, plus teaching, plus dancing. It's too much. Why don't you give up the ballet?" he went on, falling into a familiar groove. "It's hard on you physically. You have no body fat. You don't even have regular menstrual cycles."

"This is not dancing's fault," she said, her temper flaring. "I got pregnant last time when I was dancing."

Daniel dragged himself out of bed without replying. This was a well-worn argument that seemed to have no resolution. Her final retort was the sting in the tail that always ended discussion. If he couldn't get her pregnant by making love night and day, then maybe *he* hadn't gotten her pregnant in the first place. She always stopped short of coming right out and saying so, but if he was thinking it then she must be, too.

Daniel showered and dressed and went out to the kitchen. Brianna was seated at the table in her nightie, watching the TV on the counter and munching on dry sugar-coated cereal. He snapped off the TV, ignoring her wail of protest.

"I'll make you scrambled eggs," he said. "With bacon." Brianna loved bacon. Her mass of blond curls bounced as she nodded enthusiastically.

Chloe came out just as he'd finished cooking, having showered and changed into black slacks and a periwinkle blue blouse. Her hair was pulled into a tight ponytail on top of her head and her face was free of makeup except for dark navy eyeliner that enhanced her blue eyes.

"Want breakfast?" he grunted, setting the pan on the oak table.

"Put a mat under that." She slipped a circle of pressed cork beneath the hot pan. Then she grabbed a banana and an apple from the glass fruit bowl. "Thanks, but I don't have time." She pecked him on the cheek. "See you later."

She didn't have time to eat, but she had time to chastise him. Whenever their baby-making goal was thwarted, they inevitably spent the rest of the day bickering. Daniel was getting sick of the cold war. "You probably won't. Mom's going to babysit tonight, while Rob and I go out for a beer. Maybe bowl a few lanes."

"Again?" she said, dismayed. "You went out last week."

"What am I supposed to do while you're performing? Sit at home and twiddle my thumbs?"

"I'm not dancing tonight. And if you're ever bored at home, you could always come and watch," she said, knowing full well that was the last thing he'd find entertaining. "It's not fair on Brianna always being dumped at your mom's."

Daniel glanced at their daughter. To all appearances, she was concentrating on her breakfast, but he had no doubt she was absorbing every word. "Brianna loves going to my mother's house. Don't you, Bri?"

Cautiously the girl raised her head and studied her parents, as if trying to judge what would be the most diplomatic answer.

"I know she does," Chloe admitted, before Brianna felt she had to choose who to support. "And your mom's wonderful to take her. You're right, you need to get out."

He could tell she was trying to make amends, but a few conciliatory words wouldn't ease the tension between them. They needed something to break the cycle of anger and resentment. A holiday? A romantic weekend for just the two of them? His mother would look after Brianna, but Daniel didn't think he could stand to spend an entire weekend checking thermometers and carrying out his "duty" as a husband. To think there'd been a time when he'd been desperate for her to want him to make love to her.

"Daniel?" Chloe's exasperated tone suggested this wasn't the first time she'd tried to get his attention. She stood in the doorway, jiggling her keys, a tiny frown pulling her eyebrows together. "I'm trying to ask you something."

"What?" It came out short and sharp. He sucked in breath through his teeth and ran a hand through his hair. "Sorry," he amended, trying to defuse his irritation. "What was it you said?"

"I've got to leave early today," she said, matching his overpolite tone. "The prof is putting on an extra tutorial in the lead-up to midterm exams. Can you take Brianna to school?"

Daniel's jaw clamped tight, as he considered the matter. It would mean a late start on the current job site, a new home he was already behind schedule on, thanks mainly to Chloe's busy timetable. But he could hardly complain, when he'd encouraged her to go back to school and promised to help out with Brianna. At the time, he'd assumed she'd choose between teaching ballet and a career in design, but instead she seemed determined to both study and dance, too.

"Don't grind your teeth," Chloe said automatically, tapping her foot while she waited for his answer.

"I'm not grinding," Daniel replied, trying consciously to relax his jaw. His most recent visit to the dentist had resulted in a lecture about the state of his molars. He glanced at Brianna, her head propped on her hand as she listlessly chewed a mouthful of scrambled eggs. *She* was the one who suffered most because of her parents' arguments. He stroked a hand down her hair and she gave him a wan smile that made his heart turn over. "I wish you'd told me earlier, but of course I can take Brianna. She's never a problem."

★ ★ ★

Chloe hurried out of the arts building, glancing at her watch and stuffing loose pages of handouts into her leather shoulder bag as she dodged a crowd of students moving between classes. The tutorial had gone overtime and she was late for Russian lit—

Whump! A man's shoulder caught hers, spinning her around and sending her papers flying.

"My gravest apologies, love," he said, squatting to gather up her notes from the pavement before they were trampled.

The familiar Australian accent rang in Chloe's ears as she stared down at the blond hair and the perfectly cut gray suit. "It's okay," she said, breathless. "Evan?"

His head shot up. Eyes widening, he straightened and handed back her pages while the crowd parted around them. "Chloe!"

Excitement, surprise, apprehension surged through her as she struggled to find her voice. "What…" She cleared her throat. "What are you doing here?"

"I'm in town for a conference on diseases of the third world." His gaze roamed over her and came back to rest on her face. "You look absolutely stunning."

"Oh, no. Well, thanks." Her hand touched her hair self-consciously, smoothing it into place. The buzzer rang inside the building, to mark the beginning of the next class. Reluctantly Chloe started to move away. "I have to go."

"Wait!" Evan walked with her along the path that cut diagonally across the quadrangle. "You haven't told me what you're doing on campus. Aren't you dancing anymore?"

"I'm dancing part-time and studying design, also teaching a couple of days a week. Hedging my bets, I guess you'd call it." She cast sidelong glances at him as she hurried along. His hair was shorter than the last time they'd met, and a cluster of fine lines rayed out from the corners of his eyes. She'd thought she was over him; she'd trained herself not to think of him. But now, face-to-face, he brought her pulse rate up just as he always had.

"How's Brianna?" Evan asked.

"She's great!" Chloe enthused. "She's in grade two and is already reading chapter books. I've got a picture." Chloe hunted through her shoulder bag for her wallet and brought out a school photo.

Evan's long fingers held the picture by the edges as he studied Brianna's face. "She's the spitting image of you," he said, handing back the photo. "Meet me for lunch and you can tell me all about her."

"I don't know." Chloe slotted the photo back into her wallet. Evan was someone she should avoid. He made her think treacherous thoughts about Daniel. And Lord knows, her marriage was shaky enough these days without adding Evan to the mix. "I've really got to go. I've got a class."

"The student cafeteria at twelve-thirty," Evan persisted.

"Don't you have to attend your conference luncheon?" she stalled. "I'd have thought that with your experience you'd be giving the keynote speech."

"I did that yesterday. Come on, Chloe. It's just lunch, I promise," he coaxed. "All very innocent. You can even ring up Daniel and invite him. Although I'd rather you didn't. It would completely put me off my feed to have the lumberjack glowering at me."

"You're terrible." She controlled her smile, determined not to succumb to Evan's charm. "And you know darn well he wouldn't be able to come, even if he wanted to. But I shouldn't, either."

"Why not? Surely it can't be because you're still attracted to me." He quirked one eyebrow. "Or are you?"

"Of course not!"

"Then meet me and prove you're indifferent," he replied airily.

"I don't have to prove a thing."

"Then why are you still here when you've got a class?"

She gave up and laughed aloud. "Good*bye*, Doctor!" Then without a backward glance she hurried off.

At twelve-thirty she was waiting just inside the doors of the cafeteria, trying to downplay the heady anticipation bubbling through her at the thought of seeing Evan. She was *over* him. At twelve-forty-five she was pacing the lobby, furious with herself for falling in with his plans and then getting stood up. Yes, he was fun, but he was also totally unreliable. And she was married, for God's sake. She loved Daniel, no matter how unreasonable, bullheaded and bad-tempered he was on occasion. What was she doing making a fool of herself by hanging around like some lovesick coed, waiting for a man she'd said goodbye to years ago?

Twelve-fifty. "That's it!" she muttered. "I'm leaving."

The double glass doors opened and Evan rushed in, out of breath. "Sorry, love. I was giving a talk on malaria and afterward there were a million questions. I got here as soon as I could."

Just like that, her irritation vanished. Of course Evan had a good reason for being late. She forgot sometimes, dazzled by his charm and good looks, how important his work was. "It's okay. The lines will have had a chance to thin out."

"Forget the cafeteria," he said. "Let's go downstairs to the pub. After the morning I put in, I need a drink."

Chloe noticed that he'd downed one beer and ordered another before he even looked at his hamburger, but she said nothing. He must be under a lot of pressure at these conferences. She sipped the white wine he'd insisted on buying her and listened avidly to stories of his years in the outback followed by another stint in Indonesia with *Médecins Sans Frontières*. Whenever he could, he went scuba diving, in Mauritius, Mexico, Tahiti...

Although her life sounded relatively pedestrian, Chloe filled him in on the past seven years, starting with Daniel's growing construction business. She played it up, making it sound even bigger than it was. Daniel was very good at what he did and she was proud of him.

She told Evan about Brianna becoming a sixer in Brownies and a pitcher on her baseball team, as well as about her own up-and-down career. "I'm taking art courses, now, for the day when I retire from dancing. I love teaching, and some knowledge of set design comes in handy when you're putting on your own pint-sized productions."

"It's too bad your career as a soloist was cut short," he said. "I saw you dance the other night."

"You did? How did you know I'd be performing?" Then she blushed at her eagerness. "Never mind. You probably didn't know."

"I rang the Ballet Victoria office and asked. They told me you were in the *corps*." He lifted his glass to drain his beer and she noticed he didn't wear a wedding ring. "I picked you out immediately," he went on. "You were wonderful. Such expressive hands, and your eyes..." He fell silent, as though words failed him.

Chloe drank in his praise, such a contrast to Daniel's indifference. True, Daniel had built her a studio and encouraged her to go back to work, but now that she was, he'd changed his tune. "You must have been in the front row, if you could see my eyes."

"Well—" he shrugged, as if embarrassed "—maybe I was just imagining. Or remembering." He shook his head. "It took me right back to when we met and I came to your first performance with Ballet Victoria. Last night, I fell in love with you all over again."

"You shouldn't say things like that, even if you are joking." Chloe tried to frown, but her smile persisted as she absorbed the admiration and affection she hadn't been receiving at home lately. How long had it been, she wondered, since Daniel had complimented her?

"I never joke about serious matters such as love," he said and winked. Then he rose. "Do you want another drink?"

"I shouldn't. Brianna gets out—" She broke off. It was Tuesday. Today, Brianna went to softball practice after school and Daniel picked her up on his way home.

"Just one more," he coaxed. "It's not every day an old friend comes to town."

"Don't you have to get back to the conference?"

He glanced at his watch. "I've already missed the beginning of the first afternoon session. I'll make sure I get there in time for the next." Then, before she could say anything more, he headed for the bar.

She stayed for another drink. And another. Every time she saw Evan, they seemed to end up drinking. Had he always liked alcohol so much or had years of working in desperate conditions done that to him? At least he wasn't a morose drunk. On the contrary, his laconic wit had her in stitches. They fed off each other, building ideas to their logical, absurd conclusions until Chloe's sides hurt from laughing so much.

By the time they climbed the stairs from the basement pub back into the daylight, hours later, she was unsteady on her feet. "That was fun. Whoops!"

She tripped on the top step and wobbled dangerously. Evan caught her in his arms. Laughing, she tried to back up, but he pulled her forward and she fell against him. They were both laughing now, her hands on his shoulders, his arms about her waist.

Their eyes met.

Their lips touched.

His kiss was as sweet and tempting as the apple served to Eve by the serpent. And just as impossible to resist. Her body was flooded with an aching need that the years apart had suppressed but not eliminated. Until thoughts of Daniel filtered through the haze. This was *wrong*.

Breathless, she tore herself away. "I've got to go."

"Meet me tomorrow."

"I can't."

He caught her by the hands. "Just for lunch—perfectly innocent. It'll be the last time I see you."

She wavered. "No kissing."

"I promise. Wait for me outside this building and we'll go someplace nicer." He released her hands, but held her with his eyes. "Tomorrow?"

Chloe swallowed. "Tomorrow."

Daniel heard Chloe's key in the lock and glanced up from the newspaper to the wall clock. Where had she been? He'd been home from work for hours. He'd tidied the kitchen from breakfast, helped Brianna with her homework and put a frozen casserole in the oven for dinner.

Chloe came in with a fluster of hurried explanations. "Sorry, I'm late. The tutorial went overtime and the traffic was horrendous."

"I thought your tutorial was first thing this morning." Daniel turned the page of the newspaper to local news of Victoria. She wasn't looking at him and she hadn't kissed him hello. Maybe she was still angry about their fight that morning.

"Um, that was my art history class," she said. "Then in media the prof said he'd be available this afternoon between three and four, so I thought I'd better take advantage of some extra help."

Daniel lost track of what she was saying. A news item about an international medical conference had jumped out at him. *Medical specialists from thirty countries are gathered at the University of Victoria this week, to exchange information on third world medicine…*

His chest tightened, squeezing the breath from his lungs. Chloe was humming as she moved around the kitchen getting out plates and cutlery. Her manner tonight was different; she was distracted, in a state of repressed excitement. A sickening feeling in the pit of his stomach told him she'd seen Evan.

"When you were late, I thought maybe you'd run into someone you knew," he said casually. If she admitted it, he would know he could trust her.

Chloe froze, her back to him. "Just the usual people in my classes," she said, too carefully it seemed to him. "I don't hang out with them much. They're mostly younger."

On the other hand, her reply didn't *prove* anything; it was possible Evan wasn't even at the conference. Yet Daniel's question had dampened her mood and appeared to have made her wary. Thoughtfully Daniel folded the newspaper and tossed it on the coffee table. "Are you going to the university tomorrow?"

"I have an eleven o'clock class. You know that." She banged open the oven and removed the casserole, angling her face away from him. "This is done. Can you call Brianna?"

Daniel went to the hallway leading to the bedrooms and called out Brianna's name. Then he returned to the kitchen and edged past Chloe to get water from the fridge. The tension in her was palpable. He touched her arm and she jumped. "Will you be late again tomorrow?"

Annoyance flickered across her face. "I don't know. Why?"

"I won't be able to pick Brianna up." He watched her closely, aware he was playing a trump card early in the game. But he wanted to remind Chloe of why they were together. And what the cost would be if she did anything to jeopardize their marriage. She might betray him, but he was certain she wouldn't hurt their daughter.

She threw him a quick glance. "I'll always be there for Brianna."

Chapter 8

At eleven-thirty the next day, Daniel left his job site and drove to the university. He parked in the visitors' parking lot and made his way across campus, stopping to ask directions to the arts building where Chloe had classes. He didn't know quite what he intended to do when he saw her—only that he had to know one way or the other if she was meeting Evan.

He sat under a tree a distance away from the entrance to the building, cap pulled low over his eyes and his elbows resting on his drawn-up knees. He looked, he hoped, like one of the many students dotted about the grass. The only thing that gave him away was a lack of books.

When a buzzer sounded a few minutes later, students poured from the buildings onto the paths crisscrossing the quadrangle. He spotted Chloe immediately. Her bright hair, her dancer's upright posture and her smooth, gliding walk. She had on her good sweater, the one he'd given her for her birthday last year. And since when did she wear skirts to class?

When she was twenty yards ahead, Daniel rose to his feet and followed, mingling with the students. Chloe's pace quickened as she approached a long, low building, but instead of entering she paused outside and glanced around.

Daniel ducked behind a pillar and pretended to read the notice board, peeking out occasionally to make sure she was still there. All this cloak-and-dagger stuff seemed juvenile and spying on her was just plain wrong, but he could no more leave now than he could cut off his hand.

Then he saw a blond man striding purposefully through the milling students. As he watched Evan gather Chloe in his arms every muscle in Daniel's body bunched, ready to rush out and attack. Except if he confronted them Chloe would be forced to decide between him and Evan. Daniel had heard the saying, "Never ask a question you don't know the answer to." Until recently he would have been certain she would be loyal to him, but now he wasn't sure.

He'd begun their marriage behind a façade of emotional invincibility, but the longer he maintained the image, the more his hidden vulnerability ate away his insides. Someday there might be nothing left of him. Maybe the real question was, how much was he willing to suffer to keep her?

Evan returned to the table in the corner of the off-campus pub with a glass of wine for Chloe and a beer for himself. He really wanted a Scotch, but he was forcing himself not to drink the hard stuff until after five o'clock. Some days he counted the minutes.

Not today, though. Today he had compensation and distraction all rolled into one petite package. It boded well that she'd dressed up for him, he thought, eyeing her pink lambswool sweater and black mini-skirt. He set Chloe's drink down and slid in next to her, instead of sitting opposite as she no doubt expected him to.

"You don't mind, do you?" he asked. "This way we can both look out at the view. The mountains are crystal clear today." His thigh gently nudged hers, his upper arm touched her shoulder. His body craved the touch of her with the same intensity it craved alcohol at times. Was it the potential danger that drew him or the seductive sweetness of oblivion?

"Your health," he said, clinking his glass with hers.

Chloe sipped gingerly and put her glass down. She kept glancing around, seemingly at a loss for words, uneasy.

"Are you worried someone will see you here with me?" Evan was amused by her suburban morality and at the same time aware that the lumberjack, if he found out, wouldn't hesitate to chop him down to size.

"No!" she said, too quickly. "Why should I? We're just having lunch."

"Exactly," he agreed. "Perfectly innocent."

"But you know, you shouldn't have kissed me quite so enthusiastically when we met." She frowned worriedly. "We're just friends now, after all."

Ah, poor conflicted Chloe. Did she expect him to believe that? Evan swirled the ice in his drink. "How are things with you and Daniel?"

"Great!" she said, smiling brightly. "Couldn't be better, actually. His business is growing steadily. He and Rob have taken on an apprentice and they have another two fellows that work with them regularly."

"You told me that yesterday. I meant you and him. Your personal relationship."

She averted her gaze. "We're fine. Really good."

"If you need to talk, I'm here for you."

She flashed him a quick sideways glance, then turned her gaze toward the water and the mountains and gulped down a mouthful of wine. "There's nothing, really. But thanks."

"Chloe, I still care about you. I can tell you're unhappy." He took her hand and she let him hold it. "Is your marriage in trouble? Is Daniel treating you badly?"

"My marriage isn't any of your business." She tugged her hand away and leaned back from him.

Damn, he'd pushed too hard, too fast. "I'm sure he's a great guy. A much better bet than yours truly."

Her shoulders relaxed slightly, easing her closer again. "What about you, Evan? Why didn't you ever marry?"

"The old story," he said, smiling sadly. "The one that got away and all that." Let her think he was still holding a torch for her—it was true.

Her half smile revealed a world of regrets. "If you'd only arrived at the church fifteen minutes earlier…"

He responded with a slight lift of his eyebrow, a tiny shrug, as if to express what words could not.

"Do you have a girlfriend?" she asked, glancing up at him from beneath her wispy bangs.

"I've got lots of girlfriends. That's not the problem," Evan said. "Finding the woman who can tempt me into settling down, is. I'd like to have kids someday. I just don't know if that'll ever happen." He paused. "Did you and Daniel not want to have any more children?"

"We're trying for another baby," she told him. "But we're having trouble conceiving."

"How long have you been trying?"

"Two years."

"Have you had tests?"

"One of my fallopian tubes is blocked, but the other is fine," she said. "I must be able to have a baby, since I had Brianna."

"And the lumber…I mean, Daniel?"

Chloe frowned, the first overt sign of annoyance

to mar her smooth profile. "He refuses to get tested. It's some macho thing with him. Like it's a test of his virility or something."

"Well, of course that's rubbish," Evan said, hiding his glee. "But to his sort…"

"What do you mean, *his sort?*" Chloe said sharply.

"Nothing." Evan held his hands up. She might be fed up with her husband, but she was quick to defend him. "Men who work with their hands for a living tend to define themselves by strength." Not brain power.

"He's smart enough," she said, replying to his unspoken comment. "Just pigheaded. I went to the clinic at the university this morning and got some pamphlets." She broke off to hunt through her purse.

"Yes, yes, I'm sure that'll be very helpful." Enough about the lumberjack. Evan dipped into his pocket and removed a small box stamped on the lid with the name of a prominent jeweler. "I saw this on the way back to my hotel last night and thought of you."

Chloe dropped the pamphlets back in her purse. She rested the box gingerly on her palm—as if it might contain the bomb that would blow up her marriage—but made no move to open it. "You shouldn't give me presents. It's too much."

"How do you know unless you open it?" he teased. "It might be a safety pin."

"Evan!" She laughed nervously.

He took the box out of her hands and lifted the lid. She gasped as light gleamed on a slender gold brooch set with sparkling topaz.

"It's beautiful!" she whispered. Then her eyes flooded with regret. "I'd never be able to wear it."

"You can wear it when you're with me." With hands that trembled—too annoying—he slid his fingers beneath the V neck of her sweater and pinned it on.

"No! I can't accept this, Evan," she protested, fumbling to undo the catch. She pricked her thumb and the brooch clattered onto the table as she sucked away a bright bead of blood.

"Please, Chloe." He curled his hand around hers and brought it to his lips. Then he kissed her eyes, her cheeks, her mouth. "I want you to have something of me. Something more than…"

"More than what?" she asked when he broke off.

"More than memories," he whispered. "More than fleeting moments and stolen kisses in dark pubs. I can't forget you. I never stop thinking about you."

She opened her mouth to speak and he stopped her with a bruising, passionate kiss that betrayed his hunger and need. He didn't care. Seven long years he'd burned for her. Often he'd lain in the arms of other women, but no one had surpassed what he'd felt for Chloe. Sweet Chloe.

For a moment she melted into him and he forgot where he was in the fiery need to make her his, right then, right there. Then she was pushing at him, dragging her mouth away from his, breathless.

"I can't," she cried.

Evan groaned. Not again. "You *can*. You *must*."

"No! I'm sorry. I made a mistake coming here today. I thought you were willing to be just friends," she repeated. "I have to go."

Before he could stop her, she slid out from behind the table and hurried out of the pub. Evan picked up the brooch and started after her. Then he noticed her brown leather shoulder bag hanging by its strap on the back of her chair. She wouldn't get far without her car keys.

Slowly, he sat back down. He placed the brooch back in its box and put the box inside her bag, just closing the clasp as Chloe reappeared.

Evan handed over her bag. "At least stay and finish your drink. I promise I won't embarrass you again."

"No, thank you." She slung the bag over her shoulder, then gripped the strap with both hands as if to keep herself from touching him. "I have to get home to my family."

Disappointed, Evan rose and walked her out. "I'm staying at the Empress Hotel until tomorrow night, if you change your mind."

Saying goodbye in the pub parking lot left a lot to be desired. He didn't try to kiss her, but took her hand and squeezed, letting his eyes tell her how he felt.

"I'm sorry about the way things turned out," she said, squeezing back.

"I acted inappropriately," he replied. "But only because I care so much."

"Goodbye, Evan." She leaned forward on her

tiptoes and kissed him on the cheek. Then she hurried away again, toward her car.

Evan watched until Chloe's 10-year-old Volvo turned out of the lot and disappeared in traffic. He felt like howling at the loss, just as he'd wanted to on her wedding night. Once again, she'd been snatched out of his grasp, and reach as he might, he couldn't catch hold. He refused to believe she truly loved Daniel. Necessity and obligation had bound her to her lumberjack and she was too honorable to break her vows, too kindhearted to wound.

Evan had no such qualms. Much good it would do him.

Chloe pulled onto the highway heading out of the city. A wave of relief crashed over her and scattered the vestiges of regret she'd felt at leaving Evan so abruptly. When she thought about how close she'd come to making perhaps the biggest mistake of her life, she shuddered. Evan was the past and she had to keep him there. Daniel was a good husband and father, and she owed it to him to stay true to their marriage, no matter how rocky it seemed. And she loved him, she really did.

Evan cast a spell over her, a potent mixture of sophistication and sexuality that appealed to her on a different level. Evan was like a sinfully rich dessert, whereas Daniel was plain, honest fare that sustained her day after day. One wasn't good for her; without the other she'd waste away. She didn't know why she was still tempted by Evan; she simply knew that she had to resist.

She picked Brianna up from school and headed home, listening absentmindedly to her daughter's chatter about her friends and the latest must-have, an electronic virtual pet she could carry around her neck. Giving vague replies of "maybe" and "I'll think about it" Chloe's thoughts turned to the pamphlet on fertility testing that she'd tucked inside her bag. If Daniel would only read the information, he'd see how simple the procedure was and maybe he wouldn't feel so threatened.

Daniel wasn't home when they arrived, giving Chloe time to change her clothes. Evan's sandalwood aftershave seemed to have permeated the soft weave of her wool sweater. She held the garment to her nose for one deep breath, and then threw it into the back of the closet.

Dressed in clean, comfortable jeans and an old sweatshirt, she put potatoes on to bake and tucked a couple bottles of Daniel's favorite beer in the fridge to chill. Then she took steak out of the freezer and made a mountain of fried mushrooms.

The kitchen was filled with savory aromas when Daniel got home from work. Chloe was singing along to the radio, so she didn't hear him at first. And then suddenly he was standing in the kitchen, washing his hands at the sink. She'd asked him a million times to wash up in the laundry room, but he never remembered. Tonight she bit her tongue and got him a beer.

"Did you have a good day?" She smiled as she handed him the frosty bottle.

"So-so." He reached for a hand towel and took several minutes to dry his hands thoroughly before accepting the beer. "*You* seem awfully happy."

"I…I finished my media project." She suppressed a faint shiver. An ominous atmosphere surrounded him and there was an edge to his voice. He must still be angry about this morning. Remembering the steak, she turned back to the stove.

Daniel peered over her shoulder and she could smell the faint odor of sweat and sawdust, a combination she usually found masculine and sexy. But today… Well, nothing was right today.

"Steak and mushrooms, huh? My favorite meal," he commented. "What's the occasion?"

"Nothing special," she said lightly, feeling his breath on her neck, wishing strangely that he would give her some space. "There's something in my purse I want you to see."

"What is it?" He pulled on the beer, one eye fixed on her like a bird eyeing its prey.

"Just look." She flapped her hands, shooing him away.

She watched him lift the leather flap and unzip the compartment. He frowned, as though unable to see what she wanted him to see. Impossible. He couldn't fail to notice the pamphlet. Or maybe he *had* noticed and was angry. "Before you get mad…"

She broke off as he pulled out a small tan box with gilt lettering. The blood drained from her face and suddenly she felt as though she was going to be sick. How had *that* gotten in her purse?

Daniel turned to her, holding the box up. "Is this what you want me to see?"

"No!" She rushed toward him, meaning to snatch it from his hand and throw it out the window, in the garbage, anywhere but here where it taunted her, tainted her…

Too late. He opened the box and removed the glistening gold brooch, delicate and fragile between his thumb and forefinger. "*He* gave you this."

"I don't know how that got in there," she babbled, her hands to her throat. "I gave it back. I refused to accept it. I told him no."

"Sure you did."

"Daniel, you have to believe me."

"*I saw you!*" he roared, closing his fist around the brooch and squeezing until his knuckles turned white. "I saw you in his arms, kissing him like you were going to lay down for him right there on the sidewalk."

Chloe winced. "Daniel, don't. Brianna's in her room. She can hear you."

"You're not fit to clean my boots!" He threw the brooch across the room. It struck a ceramic canister, then skittered off the counter and fell under the table.

Before Chloe's horrified gaze, he dumped the frying pan, steak and all, into the garbage and threw the bottle of beer into the sink where it broke a dirty plate.

"Daniel, calm down," she begged. He stalked toward her. Seriously alarmed, she retreated to the living room. She'd never seen him like this.

His dark features twisted into a sickening combination of fury and betrayal. His fists clenched into hard knots of hatred. "You told me you loved me. I believed you."

"I *do* love you." Tears coursed from her eyes. "Daniel, please."

"I saw you kiss him," Daniel snarled.

"Wait a minute!" Anger brought Chloe upright as what he was saying sunk in. "You were *spying* on me?"

"You still love him, don't you?" Daniel demanded, ignoring her question.

"I have certain feelings for him, an attraction," she conceded, adding hotly, "but I haven't acted on them."

"That was no friendly peck on the cheek," Daniel growled. "You're a fool to think he loves you. He didn't marry you when he had the chance."

"He came all the way back from Sudan to stop the wedding, but he didn't get here in time."

Daniel shook his head in disgust and snorted. "Evan was at the church. I saw him among the guests as you were coming up the aisle. He could have stopped the ceremony right when it was starting, but he chose not to. He didn't love you enough to give up his freedom."

Chloe gasped in surprise. Old doubts surfaced but she pushed them down, remembering instead the adoration in Evan's eyes and the passion in his voice. "You're just saying that to hurt me. You want Evan to look bad."

"Evan is a jerk. He left you, pregnant and alone."

"He's a healer, a brilliant doctor. He had important work to do." Words she'd been careful never to utter before now poured from her mouth like poison. "You're just jealous because you're not as educated—"

"Stop!" Daniel bellowed. "Stop right now!"

"You're not as exciting or interesting…"

Seeing Daniel's fists clench, Chloe flinched and lurched backward into the wall unit. A vase toppled off the shelf, glanced off her forehead and fell. Her ears rang with the sound of crystal shattering on the slate hearth. Stunned, she lifted a hand to feel her grazed temple, then stared in horror and confusion at the blood on her fingertips.

"Did you really think I would hit you?" Daniel asked quietly. "You don't know me very well."

"I…no! Oh, what's the use?" she cried. "I'm getting out of here." Pushing past him, she grabbed her purse from the kitchen and without stopping for a coat she jammed her feet into a pair of leather flats at the door.

Glancing up, she saw Brianna hovering in the doorway and she almost called for her to come. But she couldn't take her daughter, not where she was going.

All the way into Victoria, she reviewed the litany of Daniel's sins. He was always working. He wasn't trying hard enough to have a baby and he blamed her dancing for their lack of success. The injustice made her grip the wheel tighter. Worst of all, *he'd spied on her.*

This last thought filled her with righteous indignation. How could he have done such a thing? Evan would have trusted her. He would have loved and cherished her. If she'd married *him,* she wouldn't have gone to the arms of another man. She never should have married Daniel in such a hurry. If she'd only waited a little longer for Evan.

Evan had been in the church from the beginning of the ceremony.

Her stream of fury came to an abrupt end. Earlier she'd brushed off the statement as evidence of Daniel's jealousy, but now the words came back to needle her. What if they were true? That meant Evan hadn't come back to claim her for his own. Or if he had, then he'd changed his mind at the last moment. He didn't love her, not really, if he could watch her marry another man. Especially knowing she might be carrying his child.

Chloe parked on Government Street and looked

up at the Empress Hotel. The old rambling stone edifice with its copper roofs stood in the midst of a vast green lawn.

Why did Evan keep coming into her life, fanning the flames of their passion? She imagined going inside the hotel, asking the night clerk to ring his room. Evan would come down to meet her, smiling in surprise. He would open a bottle of champagne to celebrate. Before long she'd be in his arms and he'd be making love to her.

The movie reel in her head ground to a halt. Before long he would disappear again.

Besides, Evan would see the cut on her temple and assume Daniel had given it to her, no matter what she said to the contrary. She couldn't allow him to think that way of her husband.

Chloe leaned her arms on the steering wheel and rested her head there, filled with a growing sense of shame and regret. Yes, Daniel had spied on her, but didn't he have just cause? If she went up to Evan's room tonight, he would have even more reason to distrust her and she would never be able to look at herself in the mirror again.

She was tempted to call Evan down to the lobby and ask if he'd been at the church before the ceremony. But if he'd lied about it before, he could easily lie again. She'd only known him six weeks and that was a long time ago.

It didn't matter what was true back then, she decided

wearily. Seeing Evan, even innocently, was a bad idea, when her marriage was on such shaky ground.

Chloe reached for the ignition and restarted the car. She felt cold to the bone, emptied of emotion and filled with confusion. She didn't know how to face Daniel; how to convince him to keep loving her.

Putting the car in gear, she pulled onto the road in the direction of home. If her marriage was over, it wouldn't be because she'd committed adultery.

Chapter 9

*D*aniel injected a puff of compressed air into his buoyancy *compensator and followed Evan along the curving iron hull. With a charge of excitement, he recognized the giant rusted spokes of the paddle wheel that had powered the old steamship. The prow was barely visible through the gloom, roughly 150 feet away. Two pairs of divers could just be made out at the forward end of the ship, wraithlike figures in the deep.*

Daniel peered inside the gaping hole that had been the door of the wheelhouse. Across the murky interior, he could make out a gangway leading farther into the ship. Evan slipped past him through the opening and twisted around to curl his forefinger. Come on.

Daniel hesitated, then swallowed his churning fears and

followed Evan in. Silt rose in thick clouds with every beat of Evan's fins, reducing visibility to a few feet. Suddenly Daniel felt something catch on his scuba tank, yanking him to an abrupt halt. On a surge of adrenaline he tried to free himself and failed. Panic made his heart race, and his sweat glands flowed freely. Ahead, Evan disappeared into the gloom, unaware that Daniel was caught.

Daniel reached over and behind his head, feeling around for the problem and cursing the thick neoprene mitts he was wearing. The tank valve had gotten itself wedged in a rusted hole in the bulkhead. Bracing his hands against the hull, he slowly wiggled the valve free.

His heart calming somewhat, Daniel glanced at his pressure gauge. Only 500 pounds of air left. At this depth that meant he had ten minutes at most. He looked around for Evan and saw him at the entrance to the gangway. Again Evan gave him the signal, Come on. *Without waiting for a reply, Evan gave a kick of his fins and went deeper into the ship.*

Daniel captured Chloe's gaze across a candlelit table in the finest restaurant in Victoria and raised his glass of champagne. "To us. Happy anniversary."

Chloe smiled back at him, her eyes relaxed and happy. "Ten wonderful years together."

Their glasses touched with a delicate clink and they drank, still holding each other's gaze. Silently Daniel gave thanks they were still together. At times, it would have seemed like a miracle, but he knew they'd made it this far because they'd both worked hard to keep their marriage alive. Ever since that terrible time three years earlier when she'd stormed out...

Daniel still tensed at the memory of that night. She'd been gone for hours, long enough for him to begin to map out a future without her, feeling empty and sick and angry. Then, to his surprise, she'd come home and crawled into bed beside him. She'd been drained and remote, saying nothing, but somehow Daniel had known that she hadn't been with Evan.

He'd pulled her into his arms and she'd lain there, passive and icy cold. After a while she'd begun to cry and he'd continued to hold her, silent for fear of sparking another conflict and breaking the tenuous link that bound them. In the days and months that followed, there were no more angry words, no accusations, no recriminations. They treated each other like fragile glass ornaments, saying little, touching less, reducing contact to brief conversations relating to Brianna, Daniel's work or Chloe's studies. It was as if they both realized how close they'd come to breaking up and didn't want to risk anything that could lead to that end. There was no lovemaking, no talk of having another child, not a word about the future.

Gradually they'd healed. In the silence of a quiet evening in front of the fire, during a bracing walk on a rainy windswept beach, as they watched their daughter sing in the children's choir on Easter morning.

Over breakfast one day not long after that same

Easter morning, Chloe looked at him with infinite sadness and asked, "Can you forgive me?"

Daniel shrugged helplessly. "*I'm* sorry."

After that, their relationship took a subtle turn in a new direction. By mutual consent they started to do more together, taking up ballroom dancing and going for weekends on their own to Vancouver and Seattle, once to San Francisco. Daniel made an effort to accompany her to the theater and concerts, and Chloe, in turn, helped with his growing business by fielding phone calls. She'd even tried to do his bookkeeping, the basic monthly records that he later gave to his accountant to calculate income tax.

He was surprised he had to teach her how to keep the accounts straight. "I can't believe you don't know this," he said, sitting back from his calculator and ledger to stare at her. "How do you organize your ballet school accounts? Don't you keep records?

"Don't need to," she said airily. "I save all my receipts and store them in a shoe box under the bed."

Daniel stifled a smile. Then it occurred to him he'd never seen her fill out an income tax return. "Come tax time how do you sort them out?"

"I don't bother," she replied. "I pack all the receipts in an envelope with a nice note to the tax man telling him I'm hopeless with figures and ask, would he be so kind as to figure it out for me?"

Daniel shook his head in disbelief. "I don't believe it! I married an airhead."

Chloe was unfazed. "They always do it. It saves me a lot of time, unlike you, who spend hours every month doing paperwork. Plus, they don't charge a cent, which saves me accountant fees. So who's the airhead?"

Daniel had to laugh, but he decided that since his books had to be kept properly he would continue to do them himself. Her financial shortcomings aside, their relationship was solid, both as friends and lovers, the way he'd always wanted them to be.

Daniel's smile lingered on Chloe's face as he set down his glass. "You look exactly the same as the day we met."

She gave a self-deprecating laugh, but a becoming blush stained her cheeks. "I've got crow's feet."

"Laugh lines," he amended promptly.

"Aches in my knees and ankles."

"An occupational hazard."

"Yesterday, I found a gray hair!"

"Only one?" he mocked, touching the light frosting of silver at his temple. "I'm barely thirty-six and look!"

"Yes, but on you it looks sexy."

"I still can't get over how different you look with your hair short," he said. "Like you're another person."

"I thought a good haircut would give me a lift," she said, fingering the short layers. "Don't you like it?"

"It's great."

The waiter came and they ordered. Daniel spread

tapenade on a piece of bread. Why anyone would go to the trouble of mincing olives he couldn't understand, but he had to admit his horizons had broadened over the years of living with Chloe. In turn, he kept her feet firmly planted on the earth. When she wasn't leaping around on stage, of course.

"Guess what?"

"I have something to tell you."

They spoke at the same time.

Chloe laughed at the crossed conversation. "You first."

"Rob and I got the contract for the new primary school being built in west Sooke," he said. "The best part is, I'll be working close to home for a change."

"Daniel, that's wonderful. Congratulations!" Chloe exclaimed. "I'm glad for you and Rob, but also because Brianna and I will see more of you."

"Now your news," he said. "Are you thinking about going back to school again?"

After the last episode with Evan, she'd finished the semester and then she'd quit, claiming she preferred teaching to design. Daniel believed she was cutting back on her workload in an effort to revitalize their marriage. He'd appreciated the gesture and was happy that he was now in a position to repay her by spending more time at home.

"Not school." She put her hand over her glass when he started to pour her more wine. A brilliant smile suffused her features. "I'm pregnant."

Daniel couldn't speak. They'd wanted another child so badly for so long, but they'd finally given up trying, content to hang on to what they had. Tears pressed at his eyelids as he pushed his chair back and came around the table to pull her into his arms.

"Oh, Chloe," he mumbled into her neck. "I love you."

She was crying, too. "I love you. Oh, Daniel, you were right. We stopped trying so hard and it happened."

He found his way back to his seat and took both her hands in his. His face was wet with tears, but he couldn't stop smiling. "How far along are you?"

"Five weeks."

"Five weeks," he repeated wonderingly. "When did you find out?"

"A couple of days ago," she admitted. "I wanted to wait and tell you tonight."

"I wonder if it'll be a boy or a girl."

"I don't care," she said. "Do you?"

He shook his head, still dazed with delight. "We'd better start thinking of names."

Chloe laughed. "We've got a list of names a mile long. Ashley, Miranda, Emma—"

"Nicholas, James, Keith."

"You *do* want a boy!"

"No, I really don't care." Then, he grinned. "Okay, so I would like a boy—some male backup around the house might be nice at times—but I'll be happy no matter what."

"Can you build another room, or will we have to turn the dance room into a nursery?"

"There's plenty of space for an addition." His mind leapt ahead, already planning construction.

Chloe smiled blissfully. "We're going to be so happy."

The very next day Daniel started drawing up plans for the new nursery while Chloe prepared a big Sunday lunch. She'd invited her parents, Esme and Walt, and Daniel's parents, Lynn and Stan, over to celebrate the good news.

When everyone was seated and had helped themselves to food, Chloe made the announcement. "The baby is due around January fifth, give or take a week. Once I have an ultrasound, the doctor will be able to predict the date more accurately."

"Wouldn't it be wonderful if you had a New Year's baby!" Esme finished buttering a piece of crusty bread and delicately wiped her plump fingers on her napkin. "Chloe might have been born on Christmas Day, if she hadn't come two weeks early."

"To my everlasting relief," Chloe murmured. "Stan, would you like some cheese?" She passed the cheese board to Daniel's father, pondering as she sometimes did, whether Brianna took after Daniel's side of the family. Stan had salt-and-pepper hair, so he was out. Although Lynn's hair color was the product of a salon these days, Chloe knew from photos that her mother-in-law had been a natural blonde when she was younger.

"Guess you're hoping for a boy this time, eh, Daniel?" Walt's hearty voice boomed the length of the table.

"You're not on the parade ground, dear," Esme said automatically. "No need to shout."

"We've still got your electric train set in the attic, Daniel," Lynn said. "Rob and Shelly have all girls, so I've hung on to it for when you and Chloe have a boy."

"I really don't care whether we have a boy or girl," Daniel told them.

Chloe met Daniel's gaze across the table. She'd caught him the night before hunting for his old baseball mitt in the storage trunks in the garage and she'd had to remind him that Brianna was using it for softball.

"As long as mom and baby are healthy, I don't care what the gender is," Daniel insisted.

Chloe smiled. He said it so often she suspected he was trying to make himself—and her—believe it. Beneath the table, she pressed a hand to her tummy. *Whoever you are, girl or boy,* she whispered silently, *I know your daddy will love you for who you are.* Throughout her pregnancy with Brianna Daniel had been loving and supportive, but somehow he'd held back just a little, perhaps worried he couldn't love the baby wholeheartedly since he or she might not be his. But when Brianna had been born and he'd held her in his arms, Chloe had seen his face and known he'd felt unconditional love. If she had another girl, he'd feel the same again. Still, she hoped she could give Daniel a son.

"And what about you, little miss?" Lynn said to Brianna, who was sitting beside her. "Are you excited about having a baby brother or sister?"

Brianna nodded so hard it sent her ponytail bobbing. "I sure am. I need someone to help me clean up around here!"

Amid the adults' laughter, Chloe explained, teasing gently, "The poor girl has to clear the dinner table and empty the dishwasher every day. She'd like to think I'm producing a slave for her."

"Not a slave, an apprentice!" Brianna turned to Daniel for support. "Right, Daddy? I'll teach him everything I know."

Daniel laughed. "Right, kiddo."

Chloe regarded her daughter with an indulgent smile. At ten, Brianna was stretching up, growing fast. Her long coltish legs would have been graceful in ballet tights, but to Chloe's disappointment her daughter had no interest in dancing. Like Daniel, she loved the beach and the water.

After lunch and a rest, Brianna talked her grandmothers into accompanying her to the beach to watch while she went snorkeling. Chloe and the men went outside, too. While Walt and Stan sat on the back deck and talked football, Daniel paced out a third bedroom next to theirs, overlooking the water. A thick carpenter's pencil was stuck behind his ear and a dog-eared notebook peeked from his shirt pocket.

"Hold that." He handed Chloe the end of a tape

measure and walked away from her, in line with the front of the house. When he got twelve feet away he stopped and pushed a wooden peg into the soft ground. When he had all four corners measured, he ran a line of string between the pegs and sprayed fluorescent paint along the ground where he would dig the foundation.

As he worked, Chloe pulled weeds from the beds of young pansies. Their bright yellow and purple heads were a cheery addition to the evolving land-scaping. The cedar hedge at the front had filled in and the liquid amber maple they'd planted as a sapling was now a mature tree, surrounded with daffodil bulbs that bloomed every spring. The apple tree in the backyard, put in two years ago, was pink with blossoms. This year she planned to grow tomatoes along the south wall where the afternoon sun shone hot and bright.

Chloe had a barrow full of weeds when, an hour later, Brianna burst through the salal bushes. Her snorkeling mask was full of shells she'd collected, along with bits of seaweed and other flotsam, and her long ponytail was wet and dark. The two grandmoth-ers appeared soon after, huffing and panting from the climb up from the beach.

"I swear that child will be a marine biologist some day, always poking about in the tide pools." Esme glanced at the trench Daniel was digging. "Is this going to be the baby's room?"

"Oh, can't it be my room, please?" Brianna begged. "I like to look out at the water. With the binoculars I can see California sea lions on the rocks sometimes."

"How would you know a California sea lion from a Canadian one?" Esme scoffed indulgently.

"Grandma!" Brianna shook her head at the foolish question. "There are *only* California sea lions."

Chloe laughed at this exchange. "It's fine with me."

Daniel leaned on his shovel and backhanded the perspiration off his forehead. "You're the oldest," he said to Brianna. "It's only fair that you get first choice."

"Yippee! I get a room with a view." Brianna danced about, her thin arms covered in goose bumps and her teeth chattering.

"You get inside and dry off before you catch your death of cold," Lynn scolded good-naturedly as she wrapped a towel around the child. "Imagine, swimming in the ocean in May!"

Daniel wedged the dovetailed strip of oak flooring into place and hammered in a nail slantways, securing the timber. Gary, his wiry dark-haired assistant, and Randy, a brawny blond apprentice, were fitting a window, their muted voices just audible over the pop tune that blared from the portable radio sitting on the half-finished floor of the house under construction.

Daniel started to reach for another strip of oak, but then rose instead and dipped inside his shirt pocket for his cell phone. All day, he'd been unable to shake a nagging feeling he should call Chloe and make sure she was all right. There was nothing wrong that he could put a finger on, except that she'd looked tired and wan this morning—but then she often did these days. He kept telling himself it was irrational to think something would go amiss just because they wanted this baby so badly, but his growing unease had intensified to the point where he knew he wouldn't feel right until he talked to Chloe.

He punched the speed dial button for their home, checking his watch as he did so. Damn, she'd be right in the middle of her preschool class this afternoon and she didn't like him to interrupt unless it was an emergency.

"Is everything all right?" he demanded when she finally picked up on the eighth ring. In the background he could hear the tinkle of recorded piano music and the thumping of small feet.

"Fine." Chloe sounded bewildered at his abrupt tone. "Why?"

"I don't know, I just had this bad feeling." He scratched his jaw and paced, his scuffed boots sounding hollow on the plywood underfloor. "You're not tiring yourself out, are you?"

"No," she said slowly. "I'm all right."

The way she said it raised a prickle on the back of

Daniel's neck. Only two weeks had gone by since their anniversary dinner and he couldn't quite convince himself she was really going to have a baby. "There's something though, isn't there?"

"It's nothing," she assured him, but again he detected hesitation. "Just a slight discomfort in my abdomen."

"What! When did this start?" he asked, alarmed and convinced she was downplaying the problem. Dancers had to be stoic. He'd seen her definition of "slight discomfort" after a performance—toes oozing blood and torn hamstrings.

"This morning," she replied. "I really don't think it's serious."

Daniel stopped pacing in front of a window and absently scratched at the masking tape crisscrossing the pane of glass. "Any bleeding?"

"No, and the pain is only on one side."

"Could it be appendicitis?" he asked, hope warring with worry. An operation wouldn't be good, but at least it would mean there was nothing wrong with the baby.

Chloe eliminated that possibility, saying, "I had my appendix out when I was seventeen."

Daniel ran a hand through his hair. "You should see the doctor. Pain isn't good. You didn't have anything like this with Brianna."

"That's true," Chloe conceded. "I'll make an appointment as soon as my class is over."

"Good," Daniel said, but he found himself unwilling to let the matter go. "I'll come home."

"Don't you dare! I know you're under the gun to get that house finished before you start on the school." Chloe paused and he heard her give the girls instructions. "I've got to go," she told him. "See you tonight."

"Okay," he agreed reluctantly. "But if the pain gets worse, call the doctor right away."

Daniel hung up and went back to laying the floor, but his sense of unease persisted. The inane lyrics of the pop songs on the radio grated on his nerves and Gary had to tell him twice that the tiler had arrived and was about to start on the main bathroom.

Daniel glanced at his watch—another hour till knock-off. Chloe had insisted she was all right. But what if she wasn't? After waiting so long for this baby, Daniel couldn't bear the thought of anything going wrong with her or the fetus. Making a sudden decision, he unstrapped his tool belt. "Lock up when you're done," he said to Gary. "I've got to go."

"One and two and one and two. Lift your arms, twirl and step, twirl and step." Chloe's voice lilted along with the piano music, and she tried to hide her growing discomfort with a smile. Six tiny girls in pink leotards and white tights wobbled across the dance floor, chins high as they frowned in concentration. "Don't forget to look happy, ladies," Chloe reminded them. "You're having fun."

At being called ladies, the four- and five-year-olds got the giggles and their arms drooped into sagging ovals. Though Chloe knew she should be strict, she couldn't suppress her own smile. Of all her students, she loved the little ones the best.

The pain in her abdomen was worse than she'd let on to Daniel and it seemed to be increasing by the second. Ignoring it, she clapped her hands. "To the barre, please. First position. Toes wider, Alice. Tamsyn, straighten…"

She broke off as a wave of dizziness sent spots dancing in front of her eyes. Maybe she should make that doctor's appointment now, instead of waiting. But the girls were watching her expectantly, awaiting her next instruction. Drawing in a breath she carried on, as she'd been trained. "Second pos—"

Another wave of light-headedness washed over her. Good Lord, she felt as though she was going to faint. Chloe stumbled toward one of the straight-backed chairs against the far wall. Before she could reach it a stabbing pain in her belly doubled her over. With a sharp cry she sank to her knees. She glanced up to tell the girls she was all right and saw six pairs of frightened eyes staring at her.

The cramping intensified. She couldn't breathe. "Lisa," she gasped as she dropped to the floor and curled into a fetal position, "go to the kitchen. Call 911."

Lisa, a tall girl with a blond bun ran off without a

word. The rest of the children instinctively drew together while on the CD player the piano music tinkled away. The smallest girl, Molly, began to cry and sweet, chubby Samantha put her arms around her.

"Are you all right?" Tamsyn demanded. Curly-haired and green-eyed, she was the best dancer in the class.

"I'll…be…fine," Chloe said through gritted teeth. If only she'd told Daniel to come home. But she'd never dreamed it would get this bad. Cold sweat broke out all over as waves of nausea threatened to drown her. Was she going to die? She felt as if she might. Through blurred vision, she saw a dark watery stain spreading down the inside of her tights where her skirt had ridden up. What was happening to her? Was this a miscarriage?

Not the baby. *Oh, Daniel. Help.* Through the blinding pain, she worried that these little girls shouldn't see her coiled on the floor in agony.

"Go…wait…in the living room," she told them. "Call your mothers." She had no idea if they even knew their own phone numbers. Like a flock of small birds, they flitted past her on tiptoes.

The CD came to an end and stopped. Into the silence came the overloud sound of her rasping breath and her moans. *Someone, please hurry.* She felt herself drifting in and out of consciousness.

The next thing she knew, Daniel's truck was skidding to a halt in the driveway. A moment later he was kneeling beside her, his strong hands around her shoulders, pulling her into his arms.

"Chloe, Chloe, my darling," he murmured. In the background an ambulance siren wailed, coming ever closer.

"Daniel." Chloe wept, clinging to him. "I'm so sorry.... The baby."

"Don't worry, sweetheart," he whispered, trying and failing to hide the heartbreak in his voice. "Everything's going to be all right."

The paramedics arrived and gave her an injection that eased the pain and put her in a woozy state. She was vaguely aware of having her blood pressure taken and half heard the low, serious voices of the attendants as they spoke to Daniel. Then she was placed on a stretcher and loaded into the ambulance, where a paramedic got an intravenous drip going in her arm. She had little recollection of the trip to the hospital, thinking only that she couldn't die and leave Daniel and Brianna behind.

She tried to sit up, bracing herself against the weaving motion. "Brianna. Where...?"

"I called my mother," Daniel said, pushing her gently back down. "She's picking up Brianna after school. Don't worry about anything."

Chloe closed her eyes, still holding tightly to Daniel's hand and trying with all her power to shut out the pain and fear. She had to hold on. *Please God, don't let me lose my baby.*

When Chloe awoke, she was lying in a hospital bed. Although sedated, she was still in pain. Utterly weak, it took enormous effort to open her eyes and turn her head. Her senses were hyperaware; every nerve ending seemed exposed. She imagined she could hear her hair scrape loudly against the starched pillowcase. Daniel was seated in a chair next to her bed, his elbows on his knees with his head bowed and his fingers buried in his hair.

"Daniel?" she said, and it came out as a croak.

His head came up. His eyes were red-rimmed, his jaw unshaven. "Chloe," he said, reaching for her hand to kiss her knuckles. "Are you all right?"

"What happened?"

Daniel's skin pulled tight, stretching the corners of his eyes, tugging down the corners of his mouth. "You had an ectopic pregnancy. Your tube ruptured and bled." He gripped her hand harder. "We almost lost you."

"And the baby?" she whispered. Instinctively, she moved her free hand under the covers to her abdomen. She froze as she came into contact with a surgical dressing.

Daniel shook his head. "Gone."

Oh God. Not even morphine could help her now. Pain cracked the walls of her heart and spread through her body until Chloe felt as if she were disintegrating. Tears spilled from her eyes and rolled down her cheeks. The stitches on her abdomen strained against her constricting muscles. If only she'd died along with their baby. It wasn't fair that she should survive when that innocent being hadn't had a chance to live.

"Why?" she cried in an anguished whisper.

"The doctors can't be sure," Daniel replied. "You might have had an infection in the past, or your fallopian tube may have had adhesions that stopped the egg from traveling all the way down."

"Will we…" Tightness contracted her chest so she couldn't speak. Sucking in a breath, she tried again. "Will we be able to have more children?"

She read the answer in his face, though he never said a word. The wrenching pain engulfed her anew.

"It doesn't matter," he soothed, offering her a sturdy smile. "We'll be fine."

Chloe blinked, not sure she'd heard right. "What do you mean it doesn't matter? Of course it matters."

"We still have each other, and Brianna."

His stolid stoicism, his easy dismissal of their tragedy sent her mood flipping and suddenly she was furious. "We've been trying for years to have this baby. How can you tell me it doesn't matter? You wanted it just as much as I did." Her voice rose, and she dug her fingers into his hand, trying to make him understand. *"Our baby died."*

"Don't work yourself up, sweetheart." Daniel was still calm and placating, though a furrow had formed between his brows. "The nurse warned me your hormones would be all over the place."

"Don't you dare brush my grief off as hormonal!" she cried, pushing away his hand. "How can you be so unfeeling as to pretend it doesn't matter? Don't you care?"

He was silent, his mouth compressed into a thin line.

She turned away, hot tears gushing. She couldn't tell where her physical discomfort left off and her emotional torment began. Burying her face in her pillow, she sank deep into overwhelming sorrow. Dimly she heard Daniel speaking to her but she wouldn't listen, refused to understand. It was all too hard and she was so very weak. She just wanted to let go, to feel nothing—no pain, no loss, no guilt. The perspiration had cooled on her skin and now she was cold, cold right through to the bone. Blackness stole over her and she sank into oblivion.

When she awoke again she was burning up, consumed by fever. Her hospital gown was first sticky with perspiration then clammy with cold, by turns. She drifted in and out of consciousness, with no concept of time. The one constant was Daniel, always at her bedside. He spoke to her but his voice sounded far away and she couldn't make out the words.

Then one day she woke up and the raging fever was gone.

Daniel was asleep in the chair beside her bed. His beard had grown to a dark stubble, his clothes wrinkled and limp with wearing. The ache in her heart intensified. How disappointed he must be.

"Daniel?" She spoke quietly, not wanting to wake him, yet needing to hear his voice.

He blinked and automatically leaned over and pressed the back of his hand against her forehead. She got the impression he'd done that numerous times in the past days.

He breathed a sigh of relief at the feel of her cool skin. "You had an infection and they put you on an antibiotic drip. The fever's broken."

"Daniel." The tears she couldn't restrain welled in her eyes. "I'm so sorry. There must have been something I could have done to prevent this, some way to know earlier that something was wrong…"

Daniel shook his head and wiped the tears from her cheeks with his thumb. "There's no way you could have known, nothing you could have done." His sorrowful gaze met hers. "I do care, you know."

"I know."

"Part of me died when we lost our baby. I will never stop grieving for that child." He paused to take a breath. "But more than anything else, I thank God you're alive. I love you. I need you. We need to take care of each other if we're going to survive this."

Chloe moistened her cracked dry lips. "Did the doctor say whether the baby was a boy or a girl?"

Daniel's gaze turned opaque, his voice faltered. "A boy."

A boy. Daniel's dream, shattered. As was her dream of having another baby. Even though the fetus was only seven weeks old, in her mind, in her heart, in her hopes and dreams, the baby had lived and breathed, become part of their family. She'd set a place for him at the table, dressed him for school…

A sob shook her chest. "I'm so sorry."

He pressed his fingers to her lips. "Don't. Please, don't. Not when I feel so lucky to still have you."

She knew then he was right—she needed him as never before, needed his strength and love, his unwavering support and commitment.

"Hold me, Daniel, please." Tears blurred Chloe's vision. "I'm the lucky one."

Chapter 10

Daniel had no choice but to follow Evan farther into the ship. He swam over and showed Evan his pressure gauge, then spread the fingers of one hand, miming five minutes, finishing off by jerking his thumb toward the surface.

Evan nodded and then, eyebrows raised, pointed to a passageway leading toward the front of the ship. Daniel glanced at the opening and felt his chest tighten. He was too big a man for these narrow passages. He shook his head and once again gestured toward the surface. Evan held up his index finger. One minute.

Yeah, sure. Daniel showed him his pressure gauge again. No doubt Evan had plenty of air left; he wasn't hyperventilating. Evan stubbornly repeated his request for one minute, miming that Daniel should stay here.

Daniel gave in and nodded, even though leaving your buddy was the cardinal sin of sport diving. Experienced divers quite often separated to work underwater or simply to explore a wider area, but he wasn't confident enough for that and Evan knew it. But Evan also knew that Daniel wouldn't surface without him.

He watched Evan enter the passage and then set his diving watch for one minute. Another pair of divers entered the area and exchanged the okay signal. But Daniel was not okay. He could feel the regulator dragging when he sucked on it and he checked his pressure gauge again. Damn, he was low. He moved slowly around the cabin, examining the construction of the ship. From the size and location amidships, Daniel figured the room they were in could have been a dining room. Another glance at his watch showed that Evan was well past a minute, closer to three.

Where the hell was he? Daniel would run out of air soon and he'd be in serious trouble. He looked around for the other divers, but they'd moved on. With a flick of his fins he glided over to the passageway where Evan had disappeared. Daniel peered into the darkness. The light from his flashlight barely penetrated the gloom. His irritation and frustration grew. Evan might be only a few yards away around a corner and Daniel wouldn't know. It wasn't like he could yell out and get an answer.

Then he heard a faint sound coming from deep inside the ship. A metallic tapping of a diving knife against a tank. The signal of a diver in distress.

Evan. Daniel ought to let the bastard drown.

* * *

"Mom, Dad! How do I look?" Brianna's eyes sparkled with excitement as she twirled to show off her first semiformal dress in royal blue satin. The effect was marred only slightly when she wobbled on her new high-heeled shoes.

"You look like a princess." Daniel shook his head, amazed at how she seemed to have grown up overnight. He had to remind himself she was just fifteen. And all the more precious because she was their only child.

Chloe motioned at him and Brianna. "Stand together and I'll take your picture."

Daniel slipped an arm around Brianna's waist and they posed in front of the fireplace. Then he took a photo of Brianna and Chloe, marveling as he looked through the viewfinder at how similar they were. Chloe was shorter than their daughter by a couple of inches and her hair was more reddish, but otherwise they could almost have been sisters.

He drove Brianna and her date, a pink-faced boy with gelled hair named Toby, to the dance. According to Brianna, Toby was just a friend—not a boyfriend. Thank goodness for that, Daniel thought as he dropped them off. Too soon she would be falling in love and leaving home.

Time was passing too quickly. As he brushed his teeth before bed, Daniel peered into a mirror fogged with condensation from his shower and noted the visible evidence that in a couple of weeks he would turn forty. His dark hair was solidly silver around the temples now and the crease between his eyebrows had become permanent. He turned sideways to the mirror and sucked in his gut. Physical work and regular exercise kept him fit, but he wasn't twenty any more, that was for sure.

What had he done with his life? Yes, he'd built a thriving construction business, moving out of residential and into light commercial building. He and Rob had five guys working for them now, with jobs lined up a year ahead. But lately he was conscious of an emptiness, a lack of fulfillment.

Chloe was propped up in bed, reading, when he slipped under the covers a few minutes later. She looked both cute and sexy with her reading glasses perched on the end of her nose. Her firm, small breasts beckoned to him through the soft fabric of her nightgown. Daniel moved closer to nuzzle her neck and touch her gently. "You smell good."

Chloe turned a page, her attention focused on her book. "I want to finish this chapter."

With a sigh, Daniel leaned back on his pillow and massaged the bones of his wrist. On wet mornings his hands ached from years of gripping tools. Today it had poured all day and his wrist was still sore.

"Is your arthritis bothering you again?" Chloe asked without glancing over. "You should try that glucosamine I got you."

"For the last time, I don't have arthritis," Daniel

countered. Arthritis was for old men. He wasn't *that* far gone. Yet.

He had a lot to be thankful for, he reminded himself. A wife he adored; a beautiful daughter; the business, of course; and despite a few minor complaints, his health.

So why did he have this feeling the world was passing him by? Going to work, coming home, watching TV and going to bed—was that all there was to life? Most days he and Chloe fell into bed too tired to make love.

"What's happening to us?" Arms folded behind his head, he stared at the ceiling. Restlessness churned through his gut, no less urgent because he didn't know which direction he should take. But if he didn't do *something* to climb out of this rut, he would go crazy. "Every day is the same."

"Not that again." A page rustled as she turned it. "You worry too much. Everything's fine."

"I mean *life*," he said. "What's it all about?"

"Al-fie," she sang and chuckled to herself.

Daniel glanced at her, still absorbed in her book. "Don't you ever think about missed opportunities? Don't you ever wonder if you could have had a different life?"

Chloe closed her book, folded her glasses and placed both on the bedside table. "At times I wonder how far I could have gone with my dancing if I hadn't gotten pregnant when I did. But when I think about not having Brianna and you, I know I'd make the same choices again." She turned on her side, her face inches from his. "Do you regret marrying me and raising Brianna?"

"No, not at all. That's not what I meant. I just feel like there should be something more to life. I need a challenge. I'm stagnating."

"You could take an evening class," Chloe suggested. "Learn a language, like Spanish or Italian. Then when we go to Europe someday, you can speak the lingo."

"Nah, I was never good at French in school."

"How about a cooking class? We could both go. It'd be fun to learn to cook Thai food or something."

"That doesn't strike a chord, either." Daniel sighed with the frustration of not being able to pinpoint the answer. "I want something I have a genuine interest in, that I can develop over a long period."

"The only thing for you that fits that description is the sea." Chloe placed a hand on his chest and ran her finger through the dark curls. "You've got drawers full of shells and whatnot already. Obviously beach-combing and tidal pool-gazing aren't enough. Why don't you learn to scuba dive?"

The very notion brought a mixture of excitement and dread, a fear of failure and the promise of a whole new world to explore. "I told you why."

"You can do it," she insisted. "You would have to push yourself out of your comfort zone, but isn't that what you want? It's time you did something about overcoming your claustrophobia."

Daniel snorted. "Easy for you to say."

"Okay, you're right," she said, giving up instantly. "I'm sure you'll think of something else. Knitting, perhaps, or embroidery."

"I'm wise to your tricks," he said, knowing she was trying to goad him into it. He glanced at her, filled with self-doubt. "Do you really think I could do it?"

"Duh!" Chloe looked at him as if she was amazed he would even ask. "You're the most capable man I know. If you set your mind to it, you can accomplish anything."

He raised his eyebrows. "Do you really believe that?"

"About you? Absolutely."

"Then I will." Daniel lay back and stared at the ceiling, but instead of feeling tired now he was revved up in a way he hadn't felt in years. If he failed, he could at least say he'd tried. But he wouldn't, not when he wanted it this badly. Not when Chloe believed in him. Her confidence made all the difference.

"I'm going to take up scuba diving." He said it aloud, testing the sound of the words, the fit with his personality. "I'm going to be a scuba diver."

"Yes, dear," Chloe said, yawning. "Now turn out the light and get some sleep."

Daniel turned out the light, but he stayed awake a long time. With something this big, this new, to look forward to his thoughts whirled and his blood picked up its pace. He felt positively young again.

* * *

"Bye! See you next week." Chloe waved to Tamsyn and Molly from the door of her dance studio. Three years earlier she'd moved her classes out of the house and into leased premises above a strip mall in Sooke. She watched while the girls ran down the stairs. They were ten now and the last of the preschool group to keep on with the lessons.

Chloe glanced at her watch. Just after six o'clock. Daniel would be at the pool getting ready to do his scuba-diving test. If he passed tonight, then all he had to complete would be two ocean dives and he'd get his certification. She was so proud of him for overcoming his phobia. It hadn't been easy for him, although he had become adept at masking his anxiety in front of others.

Brianna was going to a friend's house tonight for dinner, so Chloe planned to watch Daniel's test— from the rec center's observation lounge so she didn't add to his nervousness. She'd grabbed her coat to leave, when she remembered she needed to check her e-mail to see if there was any news from the artistic director of the ballet academy in Vancouver about when auditions were scheduled. Renee, a promising student in her senior class, was ready to go on to bigger things and Chloe was doing all she could to help her along.

Chloe booted up the computer and opened her Inbox, waiting impatiently as the messages appeared on the screen. Oh, good, there was an e-mail from the academy. Auditions were at the end of next month; plenty of time to get Renee ready. Quickly Chloe scrolled through the rest of her messages to see if there was anything she needed to deal with immediately.

She was about to delete a message as spam when she noticed the sender's name—Evan Cutler—and stopped short. She hadn't heard from him in years. Her mouse hovered over the delete button. No good could come of resuming contact. Then curiosity overcame her. What could he want after all this time?

With a click she opened the e-mail. The years fell away and she could almost heard his sardonic Australian drawl.

Dear Chloe, I had a spare moment so I Googled you—sounds vaguely obscene, doesn't it, darl'? To my delight I found your ballet school Web site. Is it too late for me to learn the pas de deux?

Chloe couldn't help smiling to herself. Yes, Evan, I'm afraid so.

I've finally succumbed to the lure of the Big Smoke and set up practice in Sydney, specializing in tropical diseases. Every snot-nosed backpacker who returns from Asia with a case of the runs ends up in my clinic. An annual stint performing pro bono cataract operations in Indonesia helps me maintain perspective.

I hope you're well. From your Web site photo I see you're as beautiful and graceful as ever. How is Brianna? I think of her often, and trust she's growing up happy and healthy.

Yours, whenever you want, for whatever you want,

Evan

P.S. Let me know when you divorce the lumberjack. By my reckoning, your marriage should be hitting the doldrums about now.

From old habit Chloe went straight back to the beginning and read the e-mail again. In spite of Evan's closing comments, his tone conveyed a distance from their love affair. Maybe enough time had passed that they could be friends. Chloe's fingers flew over the keyboard, tapping out a reply.

Dear Evan, Nice to hear from you. You're much too old to learn ballet, I'm afraid, but I'm glad you've settled down at last. We're all fine. Brianna is growing into a beautiful young woman and shows signs of being interested in marine science. Daniel's business is booming and I love my teaching. Contrary to your reckoning we're extremely happy together though we were never fortunate enough to have another child.

Chloe frowned over the last sentence. She didn't want even a chink of dissatisfaction to show through, which Evan could get a toehold on her emotions again. Hastily she rewrote it.

We're extremely happy and spend lots of time together.

Hmm, that sounded defensive and was actually untrue, although they'd *like* to spend more time together.

We're extremely happy together. Yes, marriages often break up once people hit their forties but that will never happen to us.

Was that a case of protesting too much? No, she really believed what she'd written. She and Daniel had their share of ups and downs, but somehow they'd always managed to hang on. Their love had grown deeper and stronger through being tested occasionally.

Chloe ended on a lighter note.

Sorry you haven't found connubial bliss. Take heart, the right woman might be just around the corner.

Love, Chloe. No, strike that. He might get the wrong idea. *Best wishes?* Too cold. *Fond regards?* Too formal.

Oh, what the hell, she thought and typed, Love, Chloe. Friends signed letters to each other that way all the time.

She was about to hit Send when she stopped again. Did she really want to enter into correspondence with Evan, no matter how innocent? After all these years, it would be like opening a can of worms that she'd barely got the lid back on the last time. But she couldn't quite bring herself to delete it, either. She saved the message in the draft folder and quickly shut down the computer.

Another glance at her watch had her scrambling. She pulled a pair of track pants over her tights and zipped a fleece jacket over her leotard against the cool fall night. As she hurried out the back door a light rain began to fall, turning the tendrils that had escaped her upswept hair into a mass of fine curls.

Fifteen minutes later, she was pushing through the door of the recreation complex and climbing the stairs to the observation lounge overlooking the pool. She ordered a coffee and found a seat. Daniel was easy to pick out—he was the oldest in the class. But he could hold his own with the younger men ranged around the edge of the pool waiting their turn. In fact, he was chatting with a girl standing beside him. She couldn't have been more than twenty, and she was blonde and pretty. She kept touching her wet hair flirtatiously and Chloe watched with increasing interest. Why, Daniel was flirting right back!

She didn't often get an opportunity to see him in a different setting, interacting with people she didn't know. She wasn't entirely sure she liked the implications of what she was seeing. Although Daniel was always warm and loving, he hadn't acted that animated with *her* in years. It made her feel a little hurt, if the truth were told.

Then it was his turn to go through his paces and Chloe forgot her pique in order to watch. Placed at intervals over the deep end, four scuba tanks were lying on the bottom. Daniel's task was to dive down, take a few breaths off one tank, move to the next tank without surfacing, and so on until he reached the far side.

It *seemed* simple enough. But Daniel had told her how during practice sessions he panicked at being underwater without a steady air supply. Adding to the discomfort was the fact that the pressure of the water pulled the wet suit tight against his throat and chest, making him feel as though his breathing, when he did get to a tank, was constricted. Even being on the bottom of the pool was disorienting to him.

Chloe saw him flex his hands and she felt her own palms grow damp in anticipation. When he took a deep breath, Chloe also took a breath and held it. Daniel dropped over the side into the water, took another breath and dove. He got to the first tank and placed the regulator in his mouth. She knew he had to breathe out to expel the water from the mouthpiece before he could breathe in, a counterintuitive move that she would have found difficult. After a moment, bubbles broke the surface and she let out a sigh. One down, three to go.

Daniel swam to the next tank. This time he seemed to be having trouble staying down. His legs thrashed as he forced his way back to the bottom, where he clung to the heavy tank in order to stay submerged. Chloe found herself holding her breath as he fumbled for the regulator. He remained at the tank for several minutes, calming himself, Chloe presumed, before moving on to the next tank. This time he was quicker, more efficient, his movements less desperate-looking. By the fourth tank, he'd mastered the task. When he broke the surface at the end Chloe was grinning as Daniel hauled himself dripping up the ladder to receive a handshake from his instructor. She was about to tap on the glass to get his attention when the blond girl ran over and hugged him.

Chloe gaped, her arm frozen in an aborted high five. Why was that girl hugging *her* husband? More to the point, why was Daniel hugging her back?

Suddenly her world tilted. Daniel had always been solid and safe, just a teensy bit more in love with her than she was with him. Now she saw him as that young blonde must see him—an attractive man still in his prime, confident and successful. And in a blinding flash of painful insight, Chloe realized how far apart they'd grown. As Brianna had gotten older and required less of their time, they'd turned more and more to their work and their separate hobbies.

For the first time it occurred to her that she could lose him. Evan had always been the silent threat to their marriage, but he was long gone and far away. What if another threat lay closer to home? As Chloe watched Daniel and the young blonde, jealousy and fear etched an acid path through her mind. She'd been too complacent. Daniel was at that dangerous age when men worried about getting older and losing their attraction to the opposite sex. He was susceptible to flattery, especially from a pretty girl who could make him feel young again.

Chloe waited for him outside the reception desk, pacing the thin carpet, barely aware of the sounds of pounding balls and running feet on the basketball court next door. A whiff of chlorinated air made her turn to see the pool door open and the divers exited in twos and threes, bulging sports bags slung over their shoulders. Daniel and the blond girl came out last. He was saying something to her about adding more weights to his belt.

Chloe moved forward like an automaton to kiss him. "Sweetheart, you were wonderful. Congratulations!" She clung a second longer than she might have otherwise, aware of the girl standing watching them.

"Thanks," Daniel said, setting her away. "I didn't know you were here."

"It's a big moment for you. I wanted to share it." Her gaze flickered to the girl.

"Chloe, this is Mandy," Daniel said. "She's going to be my buddy on our checkout dives."

"Hi, Chloe. It's nice to meet you." Mandy smiled uncertainly, glancing from Chloe to Daniel.

"Likewise." Chloe's own smile felt forced. What was that glance about? Hadn't Daniel told Mandy he was married? Okay, maybe it hadn't come up, but surely the girl couldn't help notice his wedding ring. Or maybe she didn't care. As the silence grew awkward, Chloe turned to Daniel. "I've got my car, so I guess I'll see you at home."

"I'll be there soon," Daniel replied. "I'm giving Mandy a ride home."

"Super!" Chloe backed away, her idiotic grin frozen on her face. Then she turned and all but ran out the door to the parking lot.

That night Chloe discarded her boring nightshirt in favor of a slinky nightgown Daniel had given her a few years earlier for Valentine's Day.

His eyebrows rose as she climbed into bed, smelling of rose-scented body lotion. "What's the occasion?"

She slid on top of him and trailed her hands up his chest to link them around his neck. "Do we need a special occasion to make love?"

"Not as far as I'm concerned." Daniel stroked her thighs, slipping his hands beneath the satin to span her waist and then slide upward to her breasts.

Beneath her, Chloe felt Daniel grow hard, and a small satisfied smile curled the corners of her mouth. She leaned forward to give him better access to her breasts and lowered her mouth to his.

Suddenly his hands froze. "You were jealous tonight!"

"I don't know what you mean," Chloe huffed, sitting back. "Jealous of who?"

"Of Mandy!" Daniel crowed. "Hoo boy! I can't believe it. Chloe's jealous. Will wonders never cease."

Chloe slapped him on the chest, her small hand bouncing harmlessly off his muscles. "Stop that!"

"She's pretty, isn't she?" Daniel teased. "She's nice, too. And only twenty-one."

Chloe climbed off him and flounced out of bed. "So what? What's she got that I haven't?" She turned around and shook her finger at him. "You'd better not be having an affair, or...or..."

"Or what?" Daniel asked, grinning.

"For heaven's sake, Daniel! She's only a few years older than Brianna. And you're married, in case you've forgotten."

Daniel rolled his eyes. "Oh come on, Chloe, you don't seriously believe there's anything between me and Mandy."

"I saw you from the observation lounge," Chloe said. "You were flirting with her. She hugged you."

"You're making a mountain out of a molehill."

"If it made me uncomfortable, then it's not completely innocent." Chloe turned her back on him, blinking hard.

She heard the covers being pushed back and a moment later Daniel's arms wrapped around her from behind and his bristly jaw came to rest against her cheek. The warmth, the security, the love she'd come to rely on was all there as he enfolded her in his embrace. She could hardly breathe, knowing how badly she needed him.

"I'm not having an affair."

A tear broke free and rolled down her cheek. She sucked in a broken sob. "Are you bored with me?"

Daniel turned her around and cupped her chin in one big hand, lifting her face so she met his gaze. All trace of teasing had vanished and his dark eyes were serious. "I could never get bored with you. I love you. I always will."

Chloe sniffed. "And Mandy?"

Daniel shook his head. "She's a sweet girl, but she means nothing to me. Okay, maybe I get a little ego stroke from her attention. I'm only human. But it's you I want. Only you."

He kissed her then, leaving her in no doubt that he meant what he said. Chloe poured everything she had into the kiss, letting him know she loved him, too, with all her heart and soul.

Daniel carried her back to bed and they made love. Maybe it didn't have the rush of excitement of the early days of their marriage, but it was tender and satisfying.

Yet in the back of Chloe's mind she was aware that as of tonight the balance of power between them had subtly shifted. She was vulnerable. And he knew it. She could only trust that he would never use that power to hurt her.

The next day Chloe went into the studio early and booted up her computer. She opened her Inbox, clicked on the Draft folder, then on her reply to Evan. She pressed Delete. And Delete again.

He was gone. Out of her life. Never to return.

Chapter 11

"**I** don't understand why you have to go so far away to study marine biology," Daniel argued. "We have some of the most abundant marine life in the world right here on the coast of Vancouver Island."

Brianna paced in front of him, mutinous and determined. "Australia has the Great Barrier Reef. I've been accepted by the University of Queensland. This is a huge opportunity for me. I can't believe you don't want me to go."

Daniel looked to Chloe for support. And didn't get it.

"I think she should go," Chloe declared. "Let her follow her dreams while she can. You never know what's around the corner."

"Why not just take a trip?" Daniel suggested to Brianna. "We could all go, do some diving on the reef, explore the countryside. Then Brianna could come home and go to the University of Victoria."

"With your workload, you won't be able to get away until the next millennium," Chloe reminded him.

"Dad, you don't get it," Brianna complained. "I want to *live* over there, at least for a while. I have a scholarship. I've saved money. I can pay my own way, mostly. Why are you so against me going?"

"It's too far to go on your own," Daniel said.

"If that's all you're worried about, I'll travel with her," Chloe said. "I've always wanted to see Australia."

Of course, that wasn't *all* he was worried about. He would miss Brianna. After he'd gotten his scuba certification, Chloe had convinced Brianna to do the course, as well. "I'll miss my best diving buddy."

"You've still got *Mandy*," Chloe said, rolling her eyes.

"True," he replied patiently. Chloe was only teasing, pretending to be nettled by the time he spent with Mandy. There was nothing between him and the girl but a mutual love of the sport.

So why *was* he so against Brianna moving to Australia? His gaze fell on Chloe, still lithe and beautiful at forty-two even though she fretted about her lost youth. She was awfully eager to go to Australia. Daniel shook his head, impatient with himself. Her feelings for Evan were a thing of the past. Would he never rid himself of this lingering feeling of being second best in her eyes? Of being her husband by default, instead of by choice?

There was another factor he hadn't thought of in a long time. What if Chloe confessed to Brianna on the plane that another man might be her biological father and that man lived in the very country she was moving to? Knowing Brianna, she would want to find out the truth. She would insist on Chloe taking her to Evan, doing the DNA tests. Daniel could lose wife and daughter in one fell swoop.

Then he looked at Brianna—bright, optimistic, determined. She believed implicitly that he would agree to whatever was best for her. How could he hold her back?

And Chloe—he was being downright paranoid where she was concerned. She'd shown over and over that she loved him in more ways than he could count.

"All right." He threw his hands up. "Go, with my blessing."

Later, he and Chloe went for a walk on the beach. The wind was steady from the southwest, blowing their hair back from their faces with a cool bite that made Daniel momentarily long for southern climes and balmy breezes. The crunch of their shoes in the pebbles was the only sound besides the whistle of the breeze. Offshore, a pair of cormorants floated on a log, their slim black profiles etched against the gray sea.

"We should tell her I might not be her biological father," Daniel said at last.

Chloe glanced at him sharply. "Why now, after all these years? I thought you didn't want to know."

Daniel shook his head. "I don't. It's not denial, it's…" He struggled to put his feelings into words. "Love. In all the ways that count she's my daughter. But I don't know how she'd feel if she found out the truth someday and we hadn't told her."

"How could she find out, unless someone tells her?" Chloe said. "I'm not going to. You're not. Evan has never shown the slightest interest in knowing, much less *being,* her father. I say we leave it. It's just as possible that *you're* her biological father. If we start trying to explain how we came to be married, we'll only confuse her."

Daniel nodded, relieved she'd argued so strongly against it. For Chloe, Brianna's paternity obviously wasn't an issue. "What if he runs into her? It could happen. He would recognize her name, get to talking."

"It's not likely. He lives in Sydney."

Daniel glanced at her sharply. His insides were suddenly churning, though he strove to keep his voice casual. "How do you know that?"

"I had an e-mail from him about a year ago," Chloe admitted. "He found me through my Web site and wrote to me." She met Daniel's gaze steadily. "I didn't reply."

★ ★ ★

Strapped into her seat on Qantas Flight 84, ready for the homeward journey from Sydney to Vancouver, Chloe glanced at her watch for what seemed like the millionth time. What was taking so long? The plane had made the hop from Brisbane to Sydney and after an hour stopover in the airport they'd reboarded. That was forty minutes ago, however, and there was no sign they were going to take off any time soon.

She'd left Brianna in Brisbane that morning. The past two weeks had been spent moving her into her university residence, buying textbooks, confirming courses, exploring the campus and the city. Their tearful departure had left Chloe in a welter of emotions—sadness at saying goodbye, pride in her daughter's independence and more than a touch of envy. Brianna was just starting out in life and had a boundless, exciting future ahead of her. For Chloe, her youth had passed and she was settling into middle age. Where had the years gone, and all her youthful dreams?

She couldn't complain. She had a wonderful husband and daughter, she loved teaching ballet and she lived in a beautiful part of the world in solid comfort, if not luxury. So what if it wasn't the life she'd once expected—principal dancer for a major ballet company, world travel, Evan.

Stop right there, she told herself. She refused to give in to regrets, least of all over Evan. She pulled out the in-flight magazine from the seat pocket in front of her and started flipping through the pages. A moment later, the magazine lay forgotten on her lap as she stared out the window at the ground crew loading baggage onto the plane at the next docking bay. Somewhere in the city, beyond the airport, Evan lived and worked. While waiting for her plane to board she'd almost looked up his name in the phone-book. It seemed silly not to even call him. What was she afraid of?

But she hadn't called him and she was glad. Twenty-four hours from now she would be home, walking into Daniel's arms.

"May I have your attention, please," a man's voice came over the intercom. "This is Captain Phillips speaking. The delay we're experiencing is due to engine trouble. We haven't been able to resolve the problem and Flight 84 has been cancelled. After dis-embarking, please go to the Qantas desk to be placed on the next available flight. Vouchers will be distrib-uted for hotel accommodation and meals. I would like to apologize on behalf of Qantas Airways and the crew for any inconvenience."

A chorus of grumbling rose as passengers got out of their seats to retrieve their luggage from the overhead bins. Chloe filed off the plane and joined in the tedious process of lining up for a new flight and waiting for her bags to be retrieved. Luckily she was able to get onto another flight the following day.

Several hours later, she was sitting in a hotel room

in Sydney calling Daniel. "The delay is annoying," she said. "I was looking forward to getting home. We were supposed to go to the U2 concert the night I returned. I doubt you'll get a refund on the tickets. I guess you could give them to Rob and Shelly."

"Or I could ask Mandy if she wants to go," Daniel said slowly. "She mentioned how much she loves their music. She couldn't get tickets because they were sold out."

Chloe gripped the receiver. Mandy again.

"You wouldn't mind, would you Chloe?" Daniel asked.

"Of course I don't mind," Chloe said lightly, gritting her teeth.

"You should get out and see Sydney," Daniel suggested. "You said you always wanted to visit the Opera House and you and Brianna didn't have a chance on the way through."

"I suppose you're right," Chloe said, getting up to go to the window. Through gaps in the downtown buildings, she saw a tantalizing glimpse of the soaring white sails of the Sydney Opera House. "I should make the most of this time, see it as an opportunity rather than an irritation."

She said goodbye to Daniel and hung up. Then paced the room, battling her jealousy. Damn it, Mandy was only in her twenties. What could Daniel find to talk to her about? Chloe groaned. Men Daniel's age didn't associate with girls like Mandy for conversation.

Oh, this was ridiculous. Daniel wouldn't have an affair. She needed to get out and enjoy herself instead of giving in to the green-eyed monster.

Chloe changed into comfortable walking shoes, and armed with a map of the city, she set out to explore. The warm humid air was saturated with the scent of frangipani from the flowering trees that lined the street. A flock of rainbow lorikeets chattered in the branches and the forceful realization struck Chloe that she was not in her ordinary world. For the next twenty-four hours she was on her own in a foreign land, footloose and fancy free.

Avoiding the commercial center Chloe strolled through the Royal Botanic Gardens down to the waterfront. A cruise ship was just leaving the harbor, steaming past the Opera House. Both were huge and dazzling white in the brilliant sun.

She joined a tour of the Opera House, marveling at the elegance of the engineering and the beauty of the tiled roofs. There seemed to be a million steps, up and down, inside and out, multiple theaters, rehearsal and dressing rooms.

Standing in an empty row in the Concert Hall, Chloe tuned out the tour guide's spiel. With one hand on the seat in front of her, she arranged her feet in third position and extended her leg in a surreptitious *glissé*. Music filtered into her imagination, conjuring up the opening night of *Swan Lake*. The lights dimmed, the curtains rose, the strings of the orchestra swelled. The *corps de ballet* awaited their entrance in a huddle of tutus in the wings. Chloe as Odette, the Swan Queen, broke away and glided across the stage toward Prince Siegfried…

"Excuse me, ma'am. The tour ends here. Are you coming?" the guide asked from the doorway.

Chloe dropped to her heels, her cheeks warming, and glanced around. The rest of the group had already exited the building. "Yes, sorry. I…I was daydreaming."

She followed the guide back outside, blinking at the sunlight glinting off the water. What now? she wondered, scanning the tourist brochure she'd picked up at the information center. A harbor cruise, Bondi Beach, the Taronga Zoo?

None appealed. Suddenly the perfect day seemed empty all on her own. The sense of loss and dissatisfaction she'd experienced seeing Brianna in her new life gripped Chloe afresh. She felt a restless yearning for her lost youth, for the days when she might have danced on the world stage.

Aimless, she wandered around the Circular Quay toward The Rocks, where regiments of British soldiers had been stationed in the early days of the colony. Passing a darkened window, she glanced over and in the indistinct reflection saw what she wanted to see, a young woman, slim, head high, arms swinging.

An intense wave of nostalgia for the girl she'd once been washed over her. Daniel had once asked her if she had regrets for choices she'd made. Her only regrets were over things she *hadn't* done. If only she could turn back the clock—not to give up Daniel or Brianna—but to recapture that shimmering moment when the future was still unknown and everything was possible.

Dropping her brochure into the nearest garbage can, Chloe found a phone booth with an intact phone book and thrusting aside a twinge of conscience she looked up medical practitioners. She wasn't calling to resume their love affair; she simply wanted a distraction from her own thoughts. No one was better at having a good time than Evan.

With the third E. Cutler, she hit paydirt. She gave her name and told the receptionist she would hold until Evan was able to speak to her. Within minutes he was on the line.

"Chloe, is it really you?" he asked. "Where are you?"

She laughed at the surprise in his voice. "In a phone booth down at The Rocks. I'm in Sydney overnight. You see, Brianna is— Oh, I'll explain everything when I see you. Are you free later for drinks or dinner?"

"For you, I'm free anytime. Let me clear my appointment book."

"Don't you dare cancel patients," she said. "Just tell me when you'll be finished and I'll meet you."

"Okay," he conceded. "Let's say six o'clock at the Pelican Bar for drinks and we'll go from there." He gave her directions and ended the conversation on a warm note. "I can't wait to see you."

Feeling better already, Chloe walked back to the hotel. She had a facial and got her hair done. Evan remembered her with fresh, unlined skin and naturally bright hair; she didn't want him to think she'd aged badly. When she walked into the outdoor bar overlooking the harbor in a summery strapless dress and her short hair tousled into a sexy style, she felt not like a middle-aged woman but like the girl she'd once been.

Evan rose as she approached. He was as handsome as ever, blond and tanned, still in good shape, with no sign of the paunch that so many men developed in their forties.

He embraced her lightly, then stood back and let his gaze roam over her. "You look stunning, as always."

"'Flattery's the food of fools,'" Chloe remarked demurely as she took a seat with a view of the water.

"'Yet now and then your men of wit, will condescend to take a bit,'" Evan quoted in return. "Women, of course, are more discerning."

And just like that they slipped into the easy banter they'd enjoyed in the old days. Evan's open admiration of her appearance, his complete absorption in her every utterance, his instant attention to her slightest whim lifted Chloe's spirits as high as the stars and bore her aloft on a wave of laughter through the long, balmy evening.

As usual with Evan she drank too much, but for

once she didn't care. The alcohol loosened her inhibitions. The euphoria, the loss of control, suited her reckless mood. She hardly recognized herself, flirting with him, inviting his touch.

It was long after midnight when they left the restaurant. Evan linked her arm through his as they strolled back to the parking lot where he'd left his car. "I e-mailed you a year ago, but I didn't receive a reply. Did I get the wrong address?"

"No, you didn't get it wrong," she replied. "I didn't see any point in starting up a correspondence."

The warm breeze off the harbor stirred his hair as he turned to face her. "Then why did you call me today?"

"Because…" She spread her hands as if to gather her scattered thoughts. "Because I'd unexpectedly been handed twenty-four hours in which I had no responsibilities. A day between worlds, where I could be whoever I want for a brief space of time." She smiled. "It's almost as though the real me doesn't exist."

Evan cocked his head on the side. "Except that the beautiful, sophisticated woman standing before me *is* the real you."

Chloe raised her arms and dropped them, acknowledging the compliment and the unspoken kernel of truth. "She's a part of me I've suppressed for years. All I know is, I'm here for a day. Once I'm gone, I won't see you again."

His knowing smile raised a shiver deep in her belly. "Then we'd better make the most of the time we have. Come back to my place for a nightcap."

"I shouldn't," she demurred. "It's late and I have an early flight."

"Please come," he urged. "You can sleep on the plane."

"Well, okay. Just for one drink."

Evan lived in a town house several blocks up the hill from the harbor. The furnishings were modern, the décor featuring an assortment of curios Evan had collected on his travels—African masks, Balinese batiks, primitive pottery mixed with items he'd found scuba diving, including cloudy glass bottles, shells and sharks' teeth.

Looking around, Chloe noticed a woman's silk scarf draped over the coat rack, a lipstick left on the hall table. "Have you got a girlfriend?"

"No one special."

Chloe went through a sliding-glass door to an open deck with a view across the water to the city lights. *Daniel would like this.* The thought sprang to her mind out of the blue and was immediately followed by a surge of guilt. She thrust away those thoughts and sipped the glass of cognac Evan handed her, welcoming a return to that warm floaty place where she wasn't Chloe Bennett, wife and mother, but an idealized version of herself in her younger days.

And why shouldn't she indulge in a little fantasy?

Daniel *said* he and Mandy were only friends, but could she really know for sure? As he said, he was only human. Didn't she, Chloe, deserve some ego strokes, too?

Evan put his arms around her and kissed her neck, sending shivers across her skin. "I've missed you," he murmured, sliding his hand around to cup her breast. "I want you."

"No, Evan," she protested, even as her body quickened to his touch. "This isn't why I came here."

"Isn't it?" His blue eyes were dark and wicked. "I think this is exactly why you called me today. You've never forgotten me. You want to make love as much as I do."

"No, I…" she trailed off as he kissed her again. Her brain was clouded with alcohol. She couldn't think straight with his hands moving over her. Heat pulsed in her veins and pooled in her belly. It burned away her power to resist him.

"One night together," he whispered in her ear. "No one will ever know."

"But…Daniel—" she began, struggling with herself.

"Shh," Evan said. "Come with me."

And then he was leading her toward the bedroom, taking off her clothes. Chloe let him, giving herself up to the moment. *No one will ever know.*

Evan's chest, his arms, felt so different from what she was used to—thinner, still muscled but less solid. They tumbled onto his bed in a tangle of limbs, their mouths fused. The sheer illicitness of what she was doing made it all the more exciting. He was right, part of her had never forgotten him.

Evan was an accomplished lover, even better than when she'd known him eighteen years ago. He knew precisely where to touch her, exactly which words to whisper in her ear to thrill her. But as he moved inside her Chloe gradually became aware that something was wrong. The act had become mechanical; the magic had gone out of the evening. She concentrated on the smooth curve of his shoulders, the scent of his aftershave, desperate to retain the conviction that this man was her soul mate, that what she was doing was not only right but inevitable. Eventually she climaxed, after a prolonged effort from Evan, but she was left with a strong sense of physical and emotional dissatisfaction.

Evan rolled off to lay beside her, with one arm curving over her head. He stroked a hand against her breast and began to play with her nipple. "God, I've missed you. Do you remember…"

He reminisced about various incidents in their past then went on to talk about his practice, his sailboat, the play he'd seen last week, from which he quoted several passages. Chloe had forgotten how verbal he was, never pausing in a steady flow of words. Suddenly she missed Daniel with a sharp ache.

She pushed his hand away from her nipple. "It's a bit tender."

"Sorry, love." He laughed and kissed her cheek.

"Would you like another drink? I've got champagne in the fridge." She shook her head and he went on, "Perhaps you'd prefer more cognac? Or there's Chardonnay." She kept shaking her head. "Vodka, gin, Scotch."

"*Nothing.* Thank you. I've had more than enough alcohol." She pulled the sheets up over her breasts and turned on her side, edging away slightly. "You seem to drink an awful lot, Evan."

"I don't have a problem, if that's what you're trying so untactfully to say. I'm a doctor, I would know." He rolled out of bed and went to the kitchen.

Chloe wished she could have a shower. Instead of savoring the feeling of being made love to long and well, she felt dirty. Instead of whispered words of tenderness before falling asleep in her man's arms, she felt assaulted by verbiage. Instead of seeing herself as Evan's soul mate, she felt like little more than a diversion between drinks.

When Evan came back with an open bottle of champagne and glasses, Chloe was stepping into her dress and pulling it up. "I should get back to the hotel," she said. "The shuttle's coming at eight in the morning to take me back to the airport."

He poured the wine and held out a glass. "Come on, love, let's toast to being together again at last. Tonight has paved the way for the future."

Oh, God, what terrible mistake had she made? To make everything worse, the inevitable hangover had kicked in; her head was pounding and her throat was parched. Hunting for her sandals, she said, "I'm going now. If you don't want to drive me back to the hotel I'll call a cab."

His smile fading, Evan set aside the glasses. "If you must go, I'll drive you."

She found her sandals and slipped them on. "I meant what I said earlier, this was a once-off. It can't impinge on the rest of our lives."

"You can't undo what we've done," Evan said. "I only gave you what you wanted."

Filled with shame, Chloe grabbed her purse. The spell Evan had cast over her decades ago was well and truly broken. The sooner she was out of here, the better. "I was kidding myself thinking that I could sleep with you and that it wouldn't matter to my marriage," she said, tears pressing the backs of her eyes. "You said no one would know. But *I* know."

She waited for Evan at the door, watching while he put on his expensive leather jacket. "You're a long way from the refugee camps now."

"I've paid my dues." He shrugged it off, then turned to her. "Chloe, love," he said softly. "Let's not part with bad feelings. I don't know what went wrong here tonight, but whatever it is, I'm sorry."

His eyes, the soft touch on her cheek, made an eloquent appeal. Chloe felt herself soften. "It's not your fault, it's me," she said with a heavy sigh. "We had something wonderful once but circumstances changed and our lives went separate ways."

Evan snorted, releasing a whiff of alcoholic fumes.

"Circumstances! Like the small matter of your wedding to another man."

"If you'd made it to the church on time, you could have had me then." She spoke more sharply than she intended, as an undercurrent of tension and old wounds came to the surface. Evan made a noncommittal noise in his throat and she was shocked to realize he was avoiding her gaze. *Had Daniel been telling the truth?*

"*Were* you there at the church? In time to stop the ceremony, I mean?"

Evan shrugged, his face was somber. "Everything was in motion. You were minutes away from being married. How could I stop all that?"

"You could have," she cried. "If you'd wanted to."

He just looked at her.

"You *didn't* want to," she said flatly. The truth crashed upon her, flipping upside-down all the stories she'd told herself over the years.

"I didn't know what I wanted," Evan said. "Except that I wasn't ready to get married."

"I would have…" Waited. Would she? So many years later, she wasn't sure anymore. Daniel was right there when she needed him, wanting to be a father to her child, a husband to her. Would she have thrown all that away for youthful infatuation? If she'd married Evan what would her life be like now, coping with his drinking, perhaps his womanizing?

"Let's just go," she said.

As she passed the hall mirror, she looked into the

glass. Reality stared back at her with shocking clarity. She was a woman approaching middle age, with all the telltale signs—the softening jawline, the tiny wrinkles, the dull hair. Add to that the seedy morning-after look of betrayal.

She and Evan didn't speak during the long drive through the city. A hard lump of self-hatred lay in Chloe's chest, hurting like nothing had ever hurt before. She'd broken her vows to Daniel and for what? A night she wished had never happened.

Finally Evan pulled up in front of her hotel and she opened the door to get out. He put out a hand to stop her.

Chloe turned toward him, one eyebrow raised.

"I was angry back then," he began. "You'd obviously gone straight from me to Daniel."

"And you hadn't had any other women while you were in Sudan?" Her anger spilled out as fresh as if it was eighteen years ago.

"None that counted," he retorted. "None I *married.*"

"Shit." She dropped her head in her hands. Who was she to talk about staying faithful?

"For what it's worth, if I had to do it over, I would have stopped the wedding. I would have married you."

"Don't say that! I don't believe you. And anyway, it's too late." Chloe scrambled to get out of the car, barely restraining herself from slamming it shut. "*Goodbye,* Evan."

Chapter 12

*T*ap, tap, tap. The thin metallic sound increased in urgency from within the depths of the shipwreck. Daniel glanced around, but there were no other divers in sight. As much as he hated the man, Evan was his responsibility.

Breathing from his near empty tank was getting harder and harder. If he was going after Evan he didn't have a moment to lose. Gripping the door frame with both hands, he pushed through into the narrow gangway.

His flashlight barely penetrated the darkness. Every instinct he possessed screamed resistance as he forced himself to proceed deeper into the enclosed space. His chest tightened. Claustrophobia squeezed its hands around his throat.

He came to an intersecting passage and paused, listening, trying to pinpoint the direction of the tapping amid a labyrinth of gangways, holds and cabins. It seemed to be coming from the starboard quarter. He set off again, moving more slowly, peering into cabins rather than entering them, in an effort to conserve what little air he had left. With a spurt of relief, he realized the tapping was growing louder.

Daniel rounded a bulkhead and saw Evan. The other man had his leg trapped from the knee down in rotten planking. He was tapping on his tank with his knife while with his free hand he attempted to shift the wood away from his leg.

Daniel sucked the last dregs of air from the bottom of his tank. Unsheathing his diving knife he smashed the timbers around Evan's leg in a few hard blows.

Spots danced before his eyes as he pulled Evan free of the wreckage. Bands of iron tightened around his chest. His eyes wide in desperation, he gripped Evan by the shoulder and with his last ounce of energy made a slashing motion across his throat.

Daniel stood outside the immigration gates where arriving Qantas passengers were dribbling through in ones and twos and small family groups. He craned his head for a glimpse of Chloe's bright hair. She was so small she sometimes got lost in a crowd.

Finally the doors slid open and she came through pushing a trolley loaded down with suitcases and duty-free bags. She didn't see him at first and he was struck by how pale and drawn she appeared. Of course, she'd be tired; she'd been on a fifteen-hour flight, but something seemed wrong. Yet when her searching eyes fell on him they lit with happiness and, oddly, relief. Daniel smiled to himself. Did she think he wouldn't be there?

She picked up her pace and rounded the barrier to practically throw herself into his arms. "Oh, it's so good to see you!"

"I've missed you," he whispered, holding her tight. The three weeks she'd been gone was the longest time they'd spent apart in the whole of their marriage. He held her away from him, puzzled by her sudden tears. "What's the matter?"

"Nothing. I'm just glad to be home." Smiling, she wiped her eyes. "Let's go."

Chloe returned on a Friday morning and the rest of the weekend was like a cross between Christmas and a second honeymoon. She spilled out the treasures of her duty-free bags—macadamia nuts, leatherwood honey, Jack Daniel's. For the next three days they ate, drank and made love.

"You've become a sex kitten." Daniel teased as she collapsed on top of him after a surprise session in bed on Sunday afternoon. "Maybe you should go away more often." When she didn't say anything, he pushed back the silky strands of red-gold hair that had fallen over her eyes. "Hey, you in there. Can you hear me?"

She slid off him and shook her hair free. "I might grow my hair long again. What do you think?"

His eyebrows rose. She'd ignored everything he'd said. Since she'd gotten home she'd been alternately effusive and evasive. "You look fine whatever you do."

"Just fine?" she asked. "You must have a preference."

He shrugged. "It's *your* hair."

"True." She relaxed onto her back, pensively plucking at a thread in the hem of the top sheet. "I think I'll grow it."

"You lie there growing your hair. I'm going to get up," he said, pushing back the covers. "I've frittered away the whole weekend, but now I'd better go over the accounts before Monday or I'll never get it done." He paused at the door to the bathroom. "Get out any receipts from your trip. I'll check the credit card statement while I'm at it."

He was sitting at the kitchen table with invoices and receipts stacked into tidy piles when she brought out her small wad of receipts. On top was one for a tour of the Sydney Opera House. Sitting back, he watched her put the kettle on. "How was the Opera House? As impressive as it looks in pictures?"

"Better." She dropped a tea bag into the pot. "It gave me goose bumps thinking I might have danced on that stage." Then she came and sat at the table. "But that's all water under the bridge."

Daniel started sorting through the rest of her receipts. "What else did you do while you were there?" When she didn't answer, he looked up. "Chloe?"

She hunched her shoulders and screwed up her

mouth. "I walked around the waterfront, had a facial, went for dinner with Evan…"

"What!" Daniel's jaw dropped.

"It was just dinner, okay?" she snapped, jumping up again. "There's no need to get all steamed up about it."

"Come on, Chloe. With Evan it's never just anything." Daniel felt the anger building inside. Would that man never leave them alone? Then he sat back and stared at his wife. This time Evan wouldn't have made contact. Chloe had to have called *him*.

"I was wandering around on my own, feeling lonely and bored," she said, adding defensively, "I called him to say hello and he suggested dinner. Why shouldn't I see him? He's an old friend."

"He's not an ordinary friend and you know it."

"Don't browbeat me!" She poured boiling water into the teapot, slammed the lid on it and wrapped her arms around herself, her back to him.

Daniel abruptly fell silent. Chloe was acting very strangely. Had something more happened with Evan that she wasn't acknowledging? Jealousy burned in his chest. He hated being made to feel weak, like a cheated-upon husband who couldn't trust his wife. Keeping his voice calm, he asked, "Did you sleep with him?"

She gave a scornful laugh, as if the suggestion was outside even the realm of fantasy and he was an idiot to imagine such a thing. "I'd have to be a fool to risk my marriage for a one-night stand."

True, but that didn't answer the question.

Daniel pondered his options. He could force the issue and demand to know exactly what she'd done every minute of the time she'd spent in Sydney. Or he could decide to trust her and let it drop. She'd told him the last time that there was nothing between her and Evan. He had to believe her or go crazy.

"What's Brianna's new roommate like?" he said, changing the subject.

Chloe sigh of relief was just audible. "She's lovely. Her name's Katie and she's from Malaysia…"

Daniel barely listened as once again he tamped down the anger and jealousy he'd been bottling up for years. If she had *anything* more to do with Evan ever again Daniel knew he would explode and their marriage would shatter into a million pieces.

Evan took a seat in Dr. Rick Westcott's office to wait, disturbed at finding himself on the unfamiliar side of the doctor's desk. He glanced at a poster depicting the different layers of skin and their associated organs. Another showed the different types of skin cancer—basal and squamous cell carcinoma, malignant melanoma.

Evan touched the bandage on his collarbone, where a mole had been excised a week ago. It was probably nothing. He'd find out in a few minutes. He got up to pace over to the window, vowing from now on to make a better attempt to be on time for appointments, especially for patients waiting on tenterhooks for critical results.

The door opened. Rick entered and folded his lanky frame into the chair behind the desk. "G'day, Evan."

Rick was a pale man in his early fifties, whom Evan had met on a kayak trip down the Snowy River a few years back. Evan never thought he'd end up consulting him in his professional role as a dermatologist, but a couple of months after Chloe had been to Sydney he'd noticed the suspicious-looking black circle on his collarbone.

"So, Rick," Evan said as he resumed his seat. "Are you entering the Murray River race this year?"

Rick glanced up from Evan's file, his gray eyes serious above his reading glasses. Today he was very much the doctor and not the fellow kayaker Evan had shared many a bottle of red wine with around a campfire. "The biopsy results aren't good."

Evan felt the blood drain from his cheeks and his fingers tightened around the arms of the chair. "Melanoma?"

Rick nodded. "The roots extended deep into the dermis, less than half a millimeter from capillaries that could potentially carry cancer cells to the lymphatic system."

"But that's good, isn't it?" Evan demanded. "You're saying it hadn't yet reached the capillaries."

"I can't be 100 percent sure about that," Rick said, carefully dispassionate. "Cancer cells may have broken off and migrated deeper, penetrating the blood vessels. I want to go back in and remove the sentinel lymph node."

"And if it has penetrated into the lymphatic system?" Evan asked, knowing all too well what the answer was.

"You'd be looking at radiotherapy, possibly chemo." Rick's expression softened. "Let's take one step at a time, shall we? There's an even chance it hasn't spread."

As Evan crawled home through the rush-hour traffic, he told himself everything would turn out fine; the cancer probably hadn't infiltrated his lymphatic system. But as he stood on his deck and gazed out at the bright sunshine and the sparkling blue harbor, all he saw was darkness. A black poison that had burrowed under his skin and was spreading throughout his body.

What was he doing with his life? His younger days working in refugee camps had had meaning, but in the past ten years he'd become just another overpaid doctor living a self-indulgent life in the city. Sure, he did pro bono work in Indonesia, but that was as much for his own sanity as it was to help the less fortunate.

He was halfway through his forties and still living as if he were a twenty-something bachelor, bringing home a different, usually much younger, woman every weekend. He'd thought he would be married and have children by now.

Chloe. If only he had spoken up at the church, all those years ago, he might have wrested her away from the lumberjack. She'd loved him. He'd loved her, perhaps not as well as she deserved, but more than he'd loved anyone else before or since.

Somehow he'd always thought he had plenty of time. Eventually her marriage had to break down, because she was so unsuited to Daniel. She would call Evan. He would go to her. They would take up where they left off. Until then his plan had been to enjoy himself while he could. But he'd ended up working too hard, drinking too much, sleeping with women whose names he couldn't remember the next day.

For all his busy life filled with pretty people, he was lonely without someone special to make it worthwhile. Now his life was hanging in the balance and it was too late to win Chloe back. Face it, he hadn't given her any reason to *want* him back.

He went to the drinks cabinet and poured himself a tumbler of neat Scotch. If ever there was a time to drown his sorrows, it was now. But as he raised the glass to his lips, he paused. What was he thinking? If ever there was a time to get *sober,* it was now. He was weary of his dissolute life. More than that, he needed to be as healthy as possible to combat the cancer.

And he wanted Chloe. Enough, finally, to marry her. This scare was a wake-up call, a chance to reassess his priorities and acknowledge what was really important in life—home, family, love.

Chloe had slept with him. That meant she still wanted him. Okay, so she'd suffered a guilt attack and retreated, but she might have gotten over that if he hadn't confessed to being at the church. The time had come for him to tell her he wanted to spend the rest of his life with her.

Evan walked over to the sink and poured the entire eighty-dollar bottle of Scotch down the sink. He would lick the cancer, give up drinking and then he'd ask—no, *beg*—Chloe to marry him.

It wasn't too late for them. It couldn't be.

"I'll let you get settled. You know where everything is." Jack set Evan's suitcase on the floor beside the bed and then ran a hand through his thinning blond hair. "As soon as you're ready, we'll head off to the dive club for a special meeting about the wreck dive." He paused in the doorway and his hand touched the base of his throat. "That thing you had... The doctors got it all, didn't they?"

"The melanoma? Yes, in the nick of time, you might say." Evan managed a brief goulish smile. "If it had grown another millimeter deeper, it could have spread throughout my body."

Jack shook his head. "Lucky break."

Evan nodded, although to his way of thinking he'd ambled through life trusting to luck for too long. It was time to take control of his future. He waited until his brother had closed the door behind him, then he went to the phone and dialed the number he knew by heart. When Chloe answered, he breathed out in relief. No quick hang-up or awkward lies were necessary. "It's me."

There was a moment's shocked silence. Then she said, "Where are you?"

"In Victoria. I came over for my niece's wedding." Evan stopped in front of the mirror above the dresser and fingered the tiny scar on his collarbone. Mainly, he was here because he'd finally figured out what really mattered in life. "Can I see you?"

"No!" she exclaimed in an urgent undertone. "I told you in Sydney it's over between us for good."

"I need to talk to you. I've had a...scare. I've changed. Please, Chloe. We meant so much to each other once. For old time's sake?" He closed his eyes, waiting. If she would agree to see him, he was sure he could talk her around.

"What kind of scare?" she asked warily.

"Cancer."

"Oh, Evan!" she exclaimed with gratifying horror and sympathy. "Are you all right?"

"I will be, if I see you." Evan resumed his pacing. Getting her back was no longer a lark and a challenge but of the utmost importance. Why had he left it so long?

"I don't know," she said, already starting to give way as he'd known she would. "Brianna came home for Christmas and she's only got another week before she goes back to university. We're really busy."

"Come up with a time and a place and I'll call you back." Before she could say anything else he hung up.

Evan unpacked his suitcase, washed and went out to find Jack. A short time later they were on the way to the dive club meeting.

The owner of the dive shop and president of the club, Bill Adams, called for attention, then introduced Dr. Ian Brown, a marine archeologist from the provincial museum.

Pushing his glasses farther onto his nose, Dr. Brown clicked on the first slide, a sepia-colored photo of an old steamship. "The *Abigail Rose* was a 260-foot-long ironclad sidewheeler from San Francisco. In November, 1862, she was steaming north with 180 passengers and twenty-nine crew when she encountered a severe storm."

Brown clicked to another slide showing a piece of rocky coastline battered by ocean swells. "She attempted to change course at the entrance to the Strait of Juan de Fuca and head east to Victoria. A strong northerly current and high winds caused her to miss the turn into the strait and she was forced onto the rocks at Carmanah Point. A section of the hull was pierced. Taking on water, the *Abigail Rose* limped eastward as far as Port Renfrew, where she finally foundered in 100 feet of water."

Dr. Brown clicked to the next slide. "This is the ship's brass bell, recovered by museum divers two years ago." Further slides showed underwater photos

of the remains of the coal-fired steamship and arti-
facts salvaged over the years. It was remarkably intact,
although overgrown with sea life.

The lights came on at the end of the slide show
and Bill Adams returned to tackle the logistics of the
dive, organizing drivers to the dive site and pairing
off buddies. Evan assumed he would be diving with
his brother Jack until Jack introduced him as "my
brother, who's not only a doctor but an accredited
scuba instructor who's dived all over the world."

Bill Adams appeared suitably impressed. "Would
you mind buddying up with one of our less-
experienced divers?"

"Sure, I guess so," Evan said, and a few minutes
later found himself being introduced to his new dive
partner. Good God, it was the lumberjack.

Daniel was even bigger than Evan remembered.
For a moment he felt a thread of fear that Daniel had
found out about him calling Chloe and had come here
to beat him to a pulp. Then he realized how unlikely
it was that Chloe would tell her husband he'd tele-
phoned.

"We meet again." Evan held out his hand, then
dropped it when Daniel kept his clenched at his side.
"How's Chloe? And your daughter—Brianna?"

"They're both fine," Daniel said brusquely. "How
long have you been in town?"

In other words, *Have you been sniffing around my
wife?*

"I just got in this afternoon," Evan said easily. "So, how many hours diving have you logged?"

"Including the course?" Daniel reflected. "Twenty-eight."

Great, he was paired with a virtual novice on a wreck dive deeper than a hundred feet. Not only would a big guy like Daniel suck his tank dry in record time, leaving too little time to explore, but Evan would have to hold the guy's hand the whole way.

His disgust must have shown in his face, because Daniel added, "I don't like it any better than you do. Let's just make sure personal issues don't get in the way."

Stay away from Chloe or else... was the only way Evan could interpret this comment. The lumberjack might be inexperienced, but he wasn't stupid.

Daniel woke up the Saturday after New Year's Day feeling like a kid on Christmas morning. A dusting of snow had frosted the fir trees and turned the grass from brown to white, but the sky was crystal clear. A perfect day for the big dive.

He dressed in jeans and a dark blue corduroy shirt and went out to put on a pot of coffee, moving quietly around the kitchen. In truth, he viewed this dive with equal parts anticipation and trepidation. Diving a shipwreck had long been a dream, but having Evan as his buddy put a distinct damper on the event. He'd hoped never to see the man again, much less share the biggest dive experience of his life with him.

He and Chloe had never again referred to her overnight stay in Sydney the year before, but that didn't mean Daniel didn't think about it and wonder what had really happened. Still, he couldn't complain. Over the past year, their relationship had been better than ever. Showing his trust in her seemed to make their marriage stronger and he'd come to the conclusion that he'd made the right decision not to question her further about Evan.

Brianna came out in her pajamas, dressing gown and sheepskin slippers. Her hair was uncombed and she clutched a wad of tissues. "I'm *so* disappointed I can't go diving with you."

"Me, too, honey." Daniel got out a frying pan and a carton of eggs. "If you get over your cold, we'll have a dive before you go back to Brisbane."

"That'd be great." She blew her nose. "*You've* got to come and dive the Great Barrier Reef with me."

Chloe emerged from the laundry room next to the kitchen with a pile of clean clothes. "So, the sleepy-heads are finally awake."

Daniel glanced over and his eyebrows rose. Although her black denim jeans and lilac pullover were casual, she was also wearing lipstick and mascara, not usual for a Saturday morning. "Going somewhere?"

As she headed down the hallway to the bedrooms, she flung over her shoulder, "Brianna and I are coming with you today, remember?"

How could he forget? For days he'd been brooding about the prospect of seeing Chloe and Evan together, and now he couldn't help wonder if the makeup was for Evan's benefit.

Forget it, he told himself, and set about making breakfast for all three of them, as well as a thermos of coffee to take to the beach.

He was in the garage getting his diving gear together when he heard a car drive up. It was probably Mandy. She'd asked for a ride because her compact car couldn't handle the rugged logging road that led to the dive site. Chloe or Brianna would likely answer the door, but Daniel kept his ear cocked toward the hallway that led to the living room just in case. With the door open, he would soon hear if someone greeted her. He took down his wet suit from its wooden hanger and folded it into his dive bag, then reached for his mask and snorkel.

The doorbell rang and he paused to listen for footsteps. He heard the door open and Chloe's voice. But the newcomer wasn't Mandy. A man spoke, too low for Daniel to make out the words. Chloe's reply sounded odd, artificially bright. Puzzled, Daniel stowed his fins inside his bag and started into the hall.

He stopped before he got to the living room, frozen by the sound of Evan saying, "Please, Chloe, hear me out."

Daniel quietly stepped closer and peered around the corner. He could see Chloe and Evan, but they were too engrossed in each other to notice him. Evan was holding her hands in both of his.

"Evan, stop," Chloe said in a low voice and tried to tug away. "Daniel's in the garage. Brianna's in her room. You shouldn't have come to the house."

"What choice did I have?" Evan replied. "You never called me back to say when you would meet me. I'm here to say my piece and I'm going to do it quickly, because we don't have much time. I've been doing a lot of thinking since last year. The evening we spent together meant so much to me—"

"Shh!" Chloe glanced around, panic-stricken. "He'll hear you."

Daniel flattened himself against the wall out of sight, his heart thudding.

"I realized after you left that I love you," Evan went on. "You have to believe me. I've never been this serious about anyone."

"Oh, Evan, maybe you *do* love me. Certainly you can't seem to stay out of my life."

"*You* came to *me* last year in Sydney, remember? No one forced you to make love to me."

Daniel's heart seemed to stop. A cold sweat broke out over his skin. His hands clenched into fists. She *had* slept with Evan. With great effort he curbed the impulse to charge out there and stop this conversation. If he did that he might never find out the whole truth.

"But you don't want a permanent relationship," Chloe went on. "You admitted so yourself."

"I've changed," Evan said. "Getting cancer made me reevaluate my priorities."

"But you're all right, aren't you?"

"Y-yes. The melanoma had migrated to a couple but not all of the lymph nodes. I've had treatment and my doctors have given me a clean bill of health. But Chloe, the real reason I came here wasn't my niece's wedding. It's to ask you to be my wife. Marry me, Chloe."

Over my dead body. Every muscle Daniel possessed tensed with the effort of forcing himself to wait and hear what Chloe had to say to Evan's outrageous request.

There was complete silence.

Daniel waited one beat, two beats. Then he peered around the corner. Evan had his arms around Chloe and he was kissing her. *So that was her answer!*

A blaze of red flashed across Daniel's vision and adrenaline leaped in his blood. With an angry growl he strode out of the hall, just as the doorbell rang again. Chloe sprang apart from Evan and ran for the door without seeing Daniel come into the room. Evan did. The gaze he turned on Daniel was cool, measured.

Daniel stopped short. Mandy came into the room chatting to Chloe about the dive. She didn't seem to notice that Chloe's cheeks were flushed and her hands were twisting together.

Daniel had no choice but to control his emotions and greet Mandy. He threw a furious glance Chloe's way, but she avoided his gaze, covering her confusion by making introductions. Within seconds, Evan and Mandy were talking about the coming dive.

Daniel headed for Chloe, intending to steer her into their bedroom and demand to know what was going on. But then Brianna came in and wanted her mother to help her find her gloves. Daniel ground his teeth. It was just as well. This wasn't the appropriate time to confront Chloe about Evan.

The last thing he felt like now was going on a dive with Evan, but no one would believe him if he suddenly wanted to pull out, not after he'd been talking about the dive for weeks. Afterward, however, there would be hell to pay.

Chapter 13

*D*aniel was on the point of blacking out when his regulator was yanked from his mouth and replaced with another. His teeth clamped down on the rubber mouthpiece. Not thinking, he sucked hard and drew in water. Choking and sputtering, light-headed from lack of oxygen, he felt Evan push on his stomach, reminding him he needed to blow out first to expel the water from the regulator. He tried again and finally he was breathing in air, huge lungfuls of the stuff, so grateful to be alive that he forgot his anxiety over being in a confined space.

Then he realized Evan was waiting for his turn at the air supply and handed back the regulator. Evan took a couple of breaths and traded off. He made the okay sign with his *fingers, eyebrows raised. Daniel okayed back. Evan gestured with an upraised thumb to the surface. Daniel nodded. As far as he was concerned they couldn't get there soon enough.*

Daniel retraced his journey through the narrow passageways, pausing now and then to take a couple of breaths off Evan's regulator. He navigated by instinct as much as memory until they came to a junction where Evan wanted to go left. Daniel looked up and recognized a piece of chain hanging from a beam. He was certain the correct path lay to the right and pointed in that direction. Evan shook his head.

Any illusion that they'd bonded over the danger they faced was quickly lost as the choice of direction became a struggle of wills. Evan's determined gaze challenged Daniel to oppose his greater experience, but Daniel stubbornly refused to follow. He took a last deep breath, gave up the regulator and swam away down the right-hand passage.

It was a gamble, but as long as he could hold his breath until he was free of the ship, then—theoretically at least—he could surface on one lungful, expelling air as it expanded in his chest with the decrease in pressure.

Daniel was feeling his lungs strain and thinking this could be the stupidest thing he'd ever done, when he felt a hand on his calf. Evan was behind him, then beside him, handing him the regulator. Their eyes locked briefly, but there was no surrender in Evan's, only a grim insistence that Daniel had better be right.

Daniel checked his watch. They were within two minutes of the absolute limit of time they could stay at this depth without risk of the bends. With no boat and anchor line to hold on to, they couldn't make a decompression stop

on their way to the surface. Even if they had enough air,
which they didn't.

He thrust his arm in front of Evan, tapping his watch.
Evan nodded and showed Daniel his pressure gauge. Two
hundred pounds of air. Could they both make it up alive?
Daniel wondered with a sick feeling in his gut.

The only thing worse than being dependent on Evan for
survival would be to die down here with him.

Chloe paced the cobbled shoreline, arms folded
tightly across her chest, her gaze fixed on the last place
she'd seen the bubbles. What could be keeping Daniel
and Evan? All the other divers had surfaced and swum
to shore. Now they were changing out of their wet
suits into dry clothes, enthusiastic about the wreck
and the sea life they'd seen.

She couldn't believe Evan had proposed marriage.
Looked at one way, she could understand how he
might think it was possible. Brianna had grown up
and left home—what was to stop Chloe from at last
being with her first love? The answer to that was her
love for Daniel, of course. Evan was not the man she'd
built him up to be in her fantasies, nor did he have
half the honesty and integrity Daniel had. This past
year with Daniel had been the best ever, a testament
to the deep bond they'd developed, initially over their
daughter and then through mutual love and respect.
For nearly two decades they'd stood together through
the difficult times and shared the joy of simple
moments.

She had to admit she got some gratification out of knowing Evan wanted her, especially after his humiliating admission that he'd deliberately let her go on her wedding day. But did he honestly think she would accept his proposal or was he just trying his luck? He hadn't even given her a chance to reply before he'd pulled her into his arms to kiss her. Thank God Daniel hadn't seen that. She hoped.

Brianna joined her mother at the water's edge. She held a tissue to her nose and blew. "They've been down an awfully long time. I hope nothing's wrong."

"Evan is an expert diver and your father is very safety-conscious," Chloe replied in an attempt to reassure them both. Given the circumstances, her efforts fell flat.

Mandy's boots crunched on the rocks as she walked over to where Chloe and Brianna were standing. Her hair was wet and there were red indentations across her forehead and down her cheeks where her mask had sealed onto her skin. She had both hands cupped around a mug of steaming coffee. "Any sign of them?"

"Not yet." Chloe hugged herself more tightly. "Did you see them down there?"

"Once, in passing," Mandy said. "It's a big ship, with lots of different decks and passageways. Plus, the visibility was poor at that depth. I'm sure they're fine."

Chloe nodded, but as Mandy returned to where the other divers were packing their gear into their bags she continued to worry. There were so many accidents that could happen during a scuba dive. What if Daniel's claustrophobia had overcome him and he'd panicked? He could have gotten lost in the ship or surfaced too fast. When this was all over they would go away somewhere, just the two of them. Someplace warm, with palm trees and romantic music and drinks with parasols.

"Look!" Brianna said, pointing out to sea. "Snorkels!"

"Where?" Chloe demanded, squinting. "I can't see."

"Halfway between the point and that freighter. See?"

"No," Chloe said fretfully. "Why didn't I bring the binoculars?" A moment later she made out the outline of first one, then two sleek black hoods. "Yes, yes! There they are!" Relief flooded through her with sweet release of the tension she'd endured for the past forty minutes.

Thank God, Daniel was safe.

Daniel banged his knees on the rocks as the ocean swell carried him onto the shore, but no pain had ever felt so welcome. He'd made it back alive. At the edge of the water Evan was already rising to his feet, fins in hand.

Buffeted by the surge, Daniel peeled off his fins and then staggered upright. As he rose from the ocean, his tank suddenly seemed to weigh a ton. The cobble shifted beneath his feet, throwing him off balance. Evan saw him stumble and held out a hand. Daniel ignored it and stepped onto firmer ground. He was dimly aware of Chloe and Brianna hurrying toward them, their faces full of relief.

"Well, mate, we made it back in one piece," Evan said.

"You're no mate of mine," Daniel ground out, unable to contain himself any longer. The man had actually proposed to his wife! This time the insult couldn't go unpunished. He swung his fist into Evan's face with all his might.

It landed with a satisfying crunch that more than compensated Daniel for the pain to his knuckles. Blood gushed from Evan's nose.

"You bastard!" Evan shouted, ripping off his gloves to feel for damage. "You bloody well broke my nose! What the hell did you do that for?"

"You know why." Daniel pushed him hard with both hands and sent Evan sprawling onto the rocks. "Now get out of my sight before I really do you damage."

"Daniel!" Chloe cried, running up to them. "Have you gone crazy? What are you doing?"

He spun and almost lashed out at her, too, the adrenaline surging through him was so strong. "We're through. Go ahead, marry him. I don't care anymore."

Brianna, close on her mother's heels, glanced from one to the other. "Mom? Daddy?"

"What are you talking about?" Chloe demanded. "I'm not going anywhere."

"Then *I'll* leave." The adrenaline drained away, leaving him deadly calm. "I heard Evan ask you to marry him."

Chloe went pale. "I didn't say yes."

"You didn't say no, either."

Evan pulled himself to his knees, blood still streaming from his nose. "She shook her head, you moron."

"But she kissed you."

"*I* kissed *her*."

"She didn't stop you." Daniel turned back to Chloe. "That's the whole problem. You never stopped him. And you slept with him in Sydney. How many other times during our marriage?"

"None!" Chloe cried. "I promise you."

"I've been living on tenterhooks for years, wondering if and when you were going to run off with Evan," Daniel said. "I'm sick of it! Our marriage, such as it is, is over. I should have ended it years ago."

"What do you mean, such as it is?" Chloe cried. "We have a good marriage. I *love* you. I don't want it to end."

"For once, Chloe, you don't have a choice."

He picked up his fins and mask, which had fallen to the ground, and started up the beach. For a while he'd thought they had a good marriage, too, but it had turned out to be full of lies. Well, this was it. Never again would he lie awake at night and wonder whom she was dreaming of.

"Yes, yes, I do," she insisted, running after him, crying. "I choose *you*, Daniel. Please don't go. Oh, my God. Daniel!"

Evan put both hands over his rapidly swelling nose and with a sharp, painful wrench moved it back into position. The blood began to flow freely again as he staggered to his feet. So it was finally over between him and Chloe. She'd chosen the lumberjack. He'd been such a fool.

Brianna stepped forward and silently held out a wad of clean tissues.

"Thanks." He'd almost forgotten she was there. He nodded with his head to Daniel and Chloe, who were nearly out of sight along the trail. "They'll be all right once your dad cools down."

"*Is* he my father—or are you?" Brianna's bright blue eyes, nearly the color of his own, regarded him with an intensity that made him want to squirm like a schoolboy.

"What makes you think I know?" He touched his nose gingerly. His whole face throbbed.

"You're a doctor. Doctors like to know medical facts."

Despite his pain he smiled at her simplistic, yet accurate deduction. She was smart, this one. He hadn't considered her feelings in this matter, but he should have—and cleared it up long ago.

"Plus you were left out of the equation when Mom and Dad married," Brianna went on. "You might reasonably want to know if the child they were raising was yours, even if you didn't want to claim me. Being a doctor, you would have found a way to do the tests."

Evan wiped his face, his blood bright red on the white tissue. There was nothing to be gained any longer from withholding that information. "I did have the tests done. You were fourteen months old at the time. I never told your mother. I thought if she remained in doubt about your paternity, it would keep alive the link between us."

"And?" Brianna probed.

"It's Daniel, of course," Evan said, conceding defeat. "He's your father."

"What about your business?" Chloe followed Daniel around the bedroom as he dragged clothes off hangers, seemingly at random, and threw them into an open suitcase on the bed. "You can't just up and leave. You've got contracts."

"It's winter—there's not much going on. Rob can handle it." Daniel crouched, to pull tennis shoes and sandals out of the closet. "He'll hire someone else, if necessary."

Chloe rubbed her hands together, shivering as if she would never get warm again. She couldn't believe this was happening. She'd talked herself hoarse this past week, but Daniel remained obdurate. His only concession had been to stay until Brianna was ready to go back to university. He would travel with her and then… "Where are you going?" she asked. "When are you coming back?"

"Brianna and I are going to dive the Great Barrier Reef. I don't know when I'm coming back, but it won't be to you." He moved past her into the ensuite bath and began going through the drawers there.

"I don't love him," she repeated from the doorway for the umpteenth time. "I love *you*."

"That's your problem."

Chloe'd thought she was cried out, but fresh tears began to fall. She blinked them away. Breaking down would do no good. Daniel was beyond being swayed by her very real grief. That was the worst thing— she'd taken the warm and loving man she'd been lucky enough to marry and turned him into someone cold and bitter.

"You don't have a ticket," she argued. "Or a visa."

"Yes, I do. I called the airline and booked a seat. I don't need a visa. Or have you forgotten that already?"

He was so cut and dried it was terrifying. Desperate to keep him with her, Chloe changed tack again. "I explained why I slept with him. It was a stupid midlife crisis. I knew right away that I'd made a mistake. Don't tell me *you* never wished you could turn back the clock. What about Mandy? Didn't you ever think about being young and free again, when you were around her?"

Daniel threw her a disdainful glance. "Maybe I thought about it, but I never *did* anything. I never would have."

"I made a mistake. A huge mistake. I was wrong. I'm sorry I hurt you. I don't know what more I can say. Please, Daniel, just don't leave. Give us a chance to work this out."

He zipped shut his suitcase and straightened, looking suddenly weary. "We've had two decades to work things out. After all we've been through it comes down to the one thing I can't forgive—you slept with him."

"It was a confusing time for me. I think I needed to find out how I really felt, whether the reality would live up to the fantasy. Maybe I needed to get Evan out of my system once and for all," Chloe said. She couldn't blame Daniel if he didn't accept what sounded like excuses, even to her. But one thing was true. "I did get him out of my system. I don't feel a thing for him anymore." She spread her hands in a gesture of finality. "It's completely over between Evan and me."

"It took you twenty years to figure out how you really feel? I deserve better than that." Daniel swung his suitcase off the bed and headed for the door. There he paused and glanced back. "It's over for us, too."

Chloe followed him to the door. Brianna was waiting there, looking uneasy. She knew Chloe and Daniel were fighting and that Daniel had made a last-minute decision to go with her to Australia, but they hadn't told her he was leaving Chloe for good.

Panic rose in Chloe's throat as she watched him load his bags into his truck along with Brianna's luggage. "Do you have your cell phone, in case I need to get in touch with you in an emergency?"

He turned, his features still frighteningly dispassionate. "I'll switch it on at noon every day for half an hour."

"What about your truck—are you going to leave it at the airport? That'll cost a bit, even for a couple of weeks." She was babbling, also revealing to Brianna that she wasn't privy to Daniel's plans, but she couldn't help herself. The longer she talked, the longer he stayed.

"Rob is going to pick it up when he's in Vancouver next week," Daniel told her.

"I see." Daniel had no further use for her. As if to prove it, he got in the truck without another word, not even a gesture of goodbye. Chloe turned to Brianna and hugged her daughter tightly. "I love you. Look after yourself and watch out for sharks."

"I will, Mom," Brianna assured her with a laugh, but she clung to Chloe a little longer. "You and Dad will be all right, won't you?"

Chloe blinked. "Of course. Don't worry about us."

Still, Brianna didn't let her go. "I asked Evan that day, on the beach."

"Asked him what?"

"Who my biological father is."

Chloe went still. "And did he know?"

Brianna nodded. "It's Dad. Evan took a sample for a DNA test when I was a baby."

The only time Evan had been around when Brianna was a baby was at the time of the choking incident. Memories of that horrible day flooded back. Of course, they'd been together at the hospital, Evan had even been alone with Brianna for a good ten minutes. What could be easier than to take a cheek swab or a hair sample?

Suddenly, Chloe was angry. He'd known all these years who Brianna's biological father was and he hadn't told her! Any last vestiges of affection Chloe held for Evan died right then and there.

Daniel started the truck's engine. She glanced at the back of his head through the rear window of the cab. "Did you tell your father?"

"I thought you would want to."

"Thank you, sweetheart." Brianna had handed her a lifeline. Or was it? Now was not the time to find out, she thought as she released Brianna. She'd never seen him so angry and hurt. This time she'd done major damage, possibly irreparable, to their relationship.

Brianna got in the truck and waved goodbye as Daniel turned out of the driveway toward the highway. Chloe waited until the truck was out of sight, then picked the newspaper off the step and went inside. She felt dazed and numb, empty inside. It was Sunday morning. She and Daniel should have been having coffee and reading the paper together. Later they would walk on the beach before visiting family or friends. Instead she was all alone in the beautiful house he'd built her.

She wandered back to the kitchen. There on the counter was the dog-eared notepad he carried with him wherever he went, containing phone numbers of suppliers, measurements, dates, cryptic scribbled notes to himself. For a moment, her heart leapt. He'd realize he'd forgotten it and come back.

Then she knew she was on the verge of cracking up. Of course he wouldn't come back for a notepad. Where he was going, he wouldn't need it. If he'd left his wife, his house and his business—his whole life—behind, there was no way he was coming back for a notepad.

She ran her thumb along the metal spiral, relishing the pain as the sharp end pricked the fleshy pad and distracted her from the pain in her heart. She'd always thought that if anyone left their marriage, it would be her. Funny how life turned out. So funny she could die from crying.

Daniel listened with only half an ear as Brianna talked about her courses, her roommate and the reef, during the drive to the ferry terminal where they would board a ship to the mainland. Chloe had begged him not to tell Brianna they were splitting up, not yet, and that was the one concession he'd made. Truth was, he didn't think he could handle the emotional scene that would follow such a revelation. Leaving Chloe had drained him completely. In order not to break down, he had to maintain an icy façade and pretend he didn't care.

"Dad, the attendant is waving you into that other lane." Brianna peered at him. "Are you all right?"

"I'm fine." He shook his head and moved into the next lane, pulling up behind a Volkswagen van.

He couldn't believe his marriage was over and with it both the crippling uncertainty and the soaring love. A dozen times this past week he'd wanted to take Chloe in his arms and forgive her. To let time and the even rhythms of their lives smooth over this rough patch, as it had on so many other occasions.

But this time was different. Something fundamental had been broken, not just his pride and his trust but his whole sense of who he was and where he belonged in the world. Chloe had been the light around which he revolved. When she'd proved inconstant, he'd spun out of orbit and drifted off into space, careering helplessly along an unknown trajectory.

He would spend a week or two with Brianna, dive the reef, get some sense of where his daughter's life was taking her. After that he didn't know. His plan was to buy a four-wheel drive and head to the outback. He'd heard men went there to lose—or find—themselves. He'd spent so long loving Chloe, being her husband that he no longer knew who he was. Maybe somewhere in the desert dust he'd figure that out.

"You are going to make up with Mom, aren't you, Dad?"

The ship's horn sounded and Daniel waited until the echoes died away. He'd promised Chloe not to tell, but he'd also promised himself no more lies. The best he could offer Brianna was uncertainty, but that was another place he never wanted to return to.

With pain that tore at his heart, Daniel replied, "No, I don't plan to. A clean break is best for us both."

Two days later Chloe was scrubbing out the cabinets under the laundry room sink when she heard the phone ring. She'd already cleaned Brianna's room and the main bathroom from top to bottom, taking everything out of the closets and cupboards in order to wash the walls and vacuum the spiderwebs out of the highest corners. She wasn't a clean freak, but the only way she could keep her misery at bay was by keeping busy. Only in that way could she obliterate the memory of the many small rituals that had comprised her daily life with Daniel.

Tossing her sponge into the soapy bucket, she peeled off rubber gloves and picked up the phone.

"I'm leaving for Sydney today," Evan said. "I wanted to say goodbye." When she didn't reply, he asked, "Chloe, are you there?"

She drew in a deep breath. "Right here where Daniel left me."

He hesitated. "Do you mean—?"

"He's gone and he's not coming back. You got what you wanted. My marriage is over."

"I'm sorry."

Amazingly enough, he did sound sorry. But that didn't exonerate him. Fury at the depth of his deception made her lash out. "Why didn't you tell me years ago that Daniel was Brianna's biological father?"

"I should have, I know. I was being selfish." His sigh was audible. "Now might not be the time to say this, but if you change your mind about me…"

"No, Evan, don't say it, not now and not ever. I'm not in love with you and I don't want to marry you." For once Chloe felt strong and resolute. She'd said similar things years earlier, but she realized now, as Evan probably had then, that she'd always been ambivalent. No wonder he'd kept coming back, when she'd sent out so many mixed signals.

"All right." He sounded defeated. After a moment he added, "You know, Daniel saved my life down there at the shipwreck. I don't know if he told you what happened."

"He didn't say anything more to me than was absolutely necessary this last week."

"Then I'll tell you," Evan said. "I went deep inside the ship and got my foot wedged in broken timber. He came and freed me."

"What was it like inside the ship?" Chloe asked. "Daniel gets claustrophobic."

"It must have been hell for him going through the dark narrow passageways to get to me. He ran out of air and we had to share my regulator then."

"He ran out of air! Oh, my God." Chloe could only imagine Daniel's anxiety, since he hadn't even mentioned the incident. Once, he would have shared every moment of the dive with her. That he hadn't even mentioned a life-and-death crisis showed just how estranged they'd become.

"What are you going to do?" Evan asked.

"I'm going to wait for him to cool down. When he's ready he'll come home. Meantime, I'm going to get on with my life." She sounded a lot more sure than she felt, but she was pumping herself up so she wouldn't break down. "How's your nose?"

"It'll heal, though I'll probably have a permanent bump in it. I suppose I should consider myself lucky he didn't break my neck." Evan paused. "Chloe, love, I really am sorry I screwed up your marriage."

"It's not your fault." She sighed. "I wrecked my marriage all by myself."

"Go after him. Go after him right away," Evan advised. "Don't wait twenty years like I did. Or you'll regret it."

Chapter 14

The road stretched endlessly in front of him, mile after mile of straight black bitumen splintered on the horizon into shimmering heat waves. On either side of the road stretched the desert—flat, featureless red dirt with tufts of spinifex grass and weird narrow trees that grew straight up. Every now and then he passed a group of wedgetail eagles feeding off kangaroo roadkill. The sky was a pale blue bowl, infinite and translucent, in which the sun blazed like a hostile all-seeing eye. For a man who'd lived his entire life beside the ocean, traveling deeper and deeper into this burning hot land was akin to entering Hell.

Daniel had driven from Brisbane north to Cairns,

where he and Brianna had spent a week diving on the Great Barrier Reef. Then he'd put Brianna on a plane and headed south and west into the outback, toward the red center of the country. The man behind the desk at the car rental place told him he was mad as a loon to be going in summer, and maybe he was. Temperatures were in excess of 120 degrees Fahrenheit and if he was stranded on an isolated track he could die of thirst before help came.

Fatalism shrouded him as he barreled down the highway, pulling out to pass road trains four semi-trailer lengths long when he couldn't see over the next rise. Day after day he waited for an oblivion that never came.

Chloe had been his life. And he'd left her. It didn't make sense, but then nothing was making sense any more. He took one day at a time, one minute at a time. Pain and loneliness were the two constants in his life. He was dead inside, burned out and hollow like the lightning-struck trees he passed along the road. He spoke only when buying gas and food at roadhouses hundreds of miles apart.

During the day pain stayed in the background. At night he lay alone in his swag in the open back of the truck and stared up at an ink-black sky encrusted with stars, feeling as if he were being devoured alive by fire ants.

Other times wind blew the desert grit against his truck windows so he had to shut them and lie there in the stifling heat, like an animal going to ground to die. Except that the next morning he would be on his way again, making sure he was fully tanked up with water and gas. His survival instinct refused to let him quit. He couldn't stop moving because moving was the only thing that was keeping him alive.

Every day at noon he turned on his cell phone. Sometimes he got a signal, but most often he didn't. Once the phone had rung and he'd clicked it on, waiting in silence. Chloe's voice said in faltering tones, "Daniel? It's not an emergency but—"

He clicked the phone off and sat there with his head down for half an hour, waiting for the sound of her voice to fade from his mind.

He pulled into Coober Pedy at seven o'clock one night, with the sun turning the wide western sky a fiery red and the locals clustered on street corners with nowhere to go. The main street resembled a frontier town on the moon. Not a blade of grass grew anywhere and only the occasional dusty shrub survived. There were few buildings, lots of junked machinery, hillocks of pale mine spoil on open lots, even the broken hull of a spaceship from a *Star Wars* movie that was used as the entrance to an underground museum. That's when he realized that most dwellings and businesses were underground and when he noted the many air shafts sticking up in otherwise vacant lots.

Coming upon a sign for a motel, he turned off the single paved street onto a gravel road that wound up a barren rocky hill. The motel was an oasis, shaded by trees and a cloth canopy that covered a barbecue and a swimming pool. As he pulled in, hundreds of chattering white parrots flew in to roost in the upper limbs of the gum trees. Daniel parked in front of the office and unfolded himself from his dusty truck.

The motel units were dug straight into the rock, with only a small covered verandah projecting out of the hillside. New excavations had been made next to the office and he paused to peer into one of the dim squared-off caverns. Stacks of lumber lay at the entrance next to the wall of smooth, porous rock. Daniel's expert eye noticed the weathering and the grit that had sifted into the cracks between the boards. For whatever reason, the lumber had lain there for a while.

"Can I help you?" a woman's voice spoke behind him.

Daniel turned to see a blond woman in her forties with an armful of towels. She was tall and strongly made, dressed in a tank top and loose cotton skirt. Her hair was bundled into a coil at the back of her head. At the base of her neck she wore a milky opal that flashed purple, turquoise and red against her tanned and freckled skin.

"Have you got a room for the night?"

"Follow me."

They pushed through the colored plastic strips that kept flies out and entered a small office. The woman set her towels on a chair and went behind the counter.

"Just the one night?" she asked, passing him a form.

Daniel nodded and she waited in silence while he wrote in his car registration and left the address section blank. No extra words, he liked that. He was sick of questions, no matter how friendly the intent. Where are you from? Where are you going? He puzzled people. His accent identified him as foreign, yet he didn't look like a tourist nor did he behave like a resident.

She gave him a key. He got his bag from the truck and went inside the unit, not quite knowing what to expect. Air vents in the ceilings whirred silently as Daniel walked through two bedrooms, a bathroom, a full kitchen and a living room complete with couch, coffee table and recliner. She must have given him a family unit. There were two small windows, one in the living room and one in the bathroom, both of which faced front. The place was quiet and somehow peaceful, kind of like being entombed.

He went to the bathroom to wash up. Rubbing soap into his hands he glanced into the mirror and took the first proper look at himself that he'd ventured in several weeks. Who was that man peering back at him? His hair was dusty and wild and it had turned salt-and-pepper all over. His skin had tanned to a deep leathery brown and his cheeks were hollow from the weight he'd lost.

He reached for a towel and found none, so he brushed the water from his eyes and dried his hands on his pants. Then he drove into town to look for something to eat. He brought a pizza and a six-pack back to his verandah and ate as the sunset died over the desert. The woman who owned the motel came out of the office and walked toward his unit carrying more towels. She moved languidly, even though the heat had faded with the sun.

"The mozzies will be out any minute," she said, coming up the steps.

"My hide is pretty thick," Daniel replied. Then, because he'd been alone so long and she didn't seem the demanding type, he added, "Want a beer?"

She hesitated, her grip tightening on the towels. Then she shrugged and gave him a smile of astonishing sweetness. "Why not? I'm Ingrid."

"Daniel."

They drank their beer in companionable silence, occasionally slapping at mosquitoes. Daniel felt himself slowly relax in her presence. She had a calmness about her that made him think about still waters. On the second beer she told him the white birds were corellas and that she'd bought the motel when her husband, an opal miner, had died in a mining accident.

"You building new units?" Daniel asked.

"Thought I was," she said with a disgusted snort. "The so-called builder took off to Adelaide a couple of months ago on a bender and hasn't been back. I can't find anyone else to finish the job. I paid the guy fifty percent in advance, too." She threw him a wry grin. "You wouldn't happen to be a carpenter, would you?"

Daniel laughed at her joke and drained his beer. "Been a long day. Guess I'll turn in."

When he crawled into bed and turned out the

light, the blackness and the silence were absolute. Instead of being eerie as he'd expected, nighttime here was peaceful. He slept better than he had for weeks, with no nightmares about running out of air or being trapped in a shipwreck. Or tapping Chloe on the shoulder and having a stranger turn around.

The next morning at dawn he stood on the verandah in nothing but his shorts to watch the corellas fly out of the trees, squawking noisily as they headed into the desert. Ingrid came out of a unit pushing a cart filled with cleaning supplies. She lifted a hand to him, then moved toward the office at her graceful leisurely pace.

Daniel put on a shirt and went down to the office. Ingrid was behind the desk, doing some paperwork. She nodded to the coffeepot and cups sitting on a low table. "Help yourself."

Daniel got himself a coffee and thoughtfully stirred in cream and sugar. "Just so happens I *am* a carpenter. Don't have my tools with me, though. Or a work visa, for that matter."

Ingrid put down her pen. "Nobody worries too much about bureaucracy out here. The carpenter left his tools behind and I kept them in exchange for what I'd already paid him. I can't afford union rates, but you can have room and board plus a reasonable wage."

"You'd hire me just like that?" Daniel tipped his head on the side. "Don't you want to know anything about me?"

She shrugged. "Let me see your hands."

Humoring her, he set down his coffee and turned his hands palm up on the desk. "Going to tell my fortune?"

Her fingertips ran lightly over his heavily calloused palms. "You're used to manual labor. That's all I wanted to know. Men come here from all over the world. The tourists stay one night, maybe two." She glanced up at him, her hazel eyes unfathomable. "The ones that are running away stay longer, sometimes a lifetime."

He met her gaze. "I won't be here a lifetime."

"Long enough to do the job is good enough for me."

He took her hand and felt the roughness of her skin and the strength of her bones. "Deal."

And as their hands and gazes held, another unspoken pact was made.

Chloe didn't go after Daniel as Evan suggested, even though a big part of her wanted to. For one thing she had no idea where on the huge continent of Australia he was. Plus she was ashamed of herself for being so pathetically weak as to first betray him and then beg him not to leave her. She couldn't have it both ways, so she was going to have to take her lumps and learn to live with the pain.

Finally, she had a business to run. Her students depended on her to show up every week and teach. The spring recital was coming up and there were new dances to learn, costumes to sew, sets to be made. She couldn't let her girls down by taking off.

She was still surprised that for the first time since she'd known him, Daniel had abandoned his responsibilities. It was so out of character. She called Rob to find out if Daniel had been in touch, expecting him to be angry at his brother's sudden absence. But instead she found Rob was accommodating and unworried.

"We sorted things out before he left," Rob told her. "I can take care of the contracts side of the business and there's plenty of carpenters around looking for work. We might suffer some because he's not around to quote on jobs or give his personal assurance of quality work, but I can live with that. He hasn't had a holiday in five years." Rob paused and added gently, "He needs time."

As one month and then two ticked by, Chloe slowly fashioned a life for herself on her own. Without Daniel to eat dinner with, or walk on the beach or talk to, she was often lonely. Then she would recall Rob's words and realize she was getting time to herself, whether she wanted it or not.

The long hours alone became a time for painful introspection. Evan, so long the third party in her marriage, was no longer an issue. In Daniel's absence new questions arose. After nearly twenty years, did she still love him or did she long for him simply out of habit? Being isolated meant they had spent most of their free time together. Who was she, when she wasn't being Daniel's wife? Did she miss him for the person he was or for the role he played in her life? If she met him now, would she fall in love with him?

She couldn't find answers to her questions, but slowly she started to fill in the empty hours. She joined a book club and took up the guitar. She renewed old friendships and strengthened new ones that might have remained superficial if not for the extra time she suddenly had on her hands. She kept the accounts for the construction business, which Rob had always left to Daniel and was happy to leave to Chloe, perhaps not realizing how out of her element she was with numbers. Still, she applied herself and didn't quit each month until the books balanced.

Esme was heartbroken over the rift. Daniel had renovated her kitchen for free and had devoured her cakes and pies with gratifying appreciation, but most of all he'd been a loving husband to Chloe and a devoted father to Brianna. Walt, on the other hand, had always supported Chloe in everything. Now he turned against Daniel, with the result that she ended up defending his abrupt departure.

Smitty, their lawyer, asked Chloe out to dinner after she told him why Daniel couldn't return his call about a lien on some property. Smitty was in his late forties and recently divorced. Chloe went out with him and found herself thinking of Daniel all the time this attractive, urbane man was telling her about a kayaking trip in Alaska. After that, she refused all invitations from him and all other men.

One warm May day, four months after Daniel had left, Chloe ran into Mandy at the drugstore. Her midriff was bare, taut and tanned between a halter top and low-slung shorts.

"Hi! Uh…" The girl obviously recognized her but had forgotten her name. "How's Daniel? I haven't seen him since the wreck dive."

"He's fine," Chloe said, smiling fiercely. She'd had to tell her family and a few others that things were amiss between them, but for some reason she wasn't ready to let Mandy know. "It's Chloe, by the way."

"Right! Sorry." Mandy tossed her hair out of her eyes. "I never did thank you for the U2 tickets. Jordan, my boyfriend, and I are huge fans. We really appreciated it."

"You're welcome," Chloe said. *Daniel hadn't gone to the concert with Mandy. He'd given the tickets to Mandy and her boyfriend.*

"Is Daniel still diving?" Mandy asked.

"Yes, in fact, he's in Australia, diving on the Great Barrier Reef with our daughter."

"Cool!" Mandy said. A lanky young man with dark blond dreadlocks came up and draped his arm loosely around Mandy's shoulder. "This is Jordan." Jordan nodded to Chloe and started to pull Mandy away. She waggled her fingers at Chloe. "I've got to go. Say hi to Daniel for me next time you talk to him."

"Sure," Chloe promised. Whenever that might be. A month from now. A year. Suddenly she found herself blinking rapidly. Yes, she'd learned she could live without Daniel but she'd also discovered how badly she missed him.

She made her purchases and drove home, feeling more melancholy than she had in a long time. The house had gradually become more and more hers. There were none of Daniel's clothes in the laundry nor did his toothbrush or shaving kit clutter the bathroom. There were no stray tools left around the house, where he'd been fixing something, and his workboots no longer sat inside the back door. During her angry stage she'd packed away everything she could find that reminded her of him. Now she went searching for pieces of Daniel to remind herself of who he was.

His shell collection was contained in a set of shallow teak drawers lined with thick felt that he'd made himself. Chloe slid open the top drawer. Rows of clam shells, marine snails, limpets, cockles and more were on display, each with a tiny slip of paper on which he'd written the common and scientific names, plus the place and date of collection.

She'd known about his collection, of course, but had never paid it much notice. Now she picked up and examined the shells one by one, marveling at how much they must have meant to Daniel for him to take such care cataloging them and learning their Latin names. He'd bought natural history books, too. A whole row of the bookcase was given over to marine flora and fauna of the Pacific Northwest.

The moon-snail shell was her favorite. The smooth, pale globe gleamed softly in her palm. She'd been with

Daniel when he'd found this on one of the island's eastern beaches. Chloe smiled, remembering the day. Brianna had been about four, chasing seagulls off the sandbars, splashing through the shallows. They'd followed the tide out for miles, finding sand dollars and moon snails galore. Brianna had wanted to carry them all home, but Daniel had taken only one small specimen for his collection. He was that way about everything. He didn't take more than he needed, yet gave all he could.

What beach was he walking now, what treasures was he finding without her on such a distant shore? Would he ever find his way back to her?

A tear fell and landed on the shell, turning the thin edge translucent. As she sat staring at it, her muddled and tumultuous feelings of the past months became clear. Daniel was her support and her champion; he grounded her and also lifted her up so she could soar. He was the well from which she replenished her spirit, the sturdy limb from which she spread her wings. Without him, she was like a bird who'd forgotten how to fly.

The time had come to find him. She wanted to tell him he was a father. She needed to offer him a divorce. Both, she felt she had to do face-to-face.

Chapter 15

Tracking down Daniel was never going to be easy. He still wouldn't answer her when she called him on his cell phone. She thought about claiming it was an emergency, but she knew that lying would be the worst thing she could do if she wanted to win him back.

The day she flew out of Vancouver, she called once more. This time, when she said she wanted to see him, she imagined a change in the quality of the silence, a charge in the atmosphere. But then he'd hung up as usual, without saying anything.

The last time he'd used his credit card was at a motel in Coober Pedy. The records showed he'd only stayed there one night three months earlier. When Chloe looked at the map and saw the hundreds of miles of desert surrounding the tiny town, her heart sank. She told herself that making the trip wouldn't be worth the trouble. Then she decided that it was the only lead she had and if there was the remotest chance the motel owner remembered him she had to try. If nothing else, she would see where he'd been; know something of what he'd experienced on his journey.

She flew to Adelaide and rented a car, driving north, with the ocean to the west and vineyards to the east. At Port Augusta the road turned inland and the land changed into a moonscape of salt flats and strange barren hills. Venturing into the outback was frightening, yet compelling, as if the environment itself was daring her to survive.

A ridiculous thought, and yet she was glad enough to pull into Coober Pedy at the end of twelve hours on the road. Desert View Motel and its parking lot had been cut out of the side of a rocky hill. Chloe got out of the car and took a moment to stretch and look around. Had Daniel felt as out of place and disoriented as she did now?

The office was dim and cool, the curved ceiling cut out of the living rock. Chloe waited until the blond woman behind the desk had served a young couple, then stepped forward. "I'd like a room for the night, please."

"Single?"

Chloe hesitated. Everything seemed a comment on her marital status and she would have to get over that. "Yes."

She filled in the form and handed over her credit card. The woman looked at it and glanced up, eyes wide. "Chloe *Bennett?*"

"That's me." Chloe was a little puzzled by her reaction. Had Daniel given the woman some reason to remember that name? "My husband came through here a few months ago. I don't know if you remember him—he only stayed one night."

"Daniel." The woman's gaze flickered away. "He stayed eight weeks."

"Eight weeks! What was he doing here all that time?" As Chloe stared, the woman's cheeks grew red. What was *that* about?

"He was building some new units," the woman said. "My carpenter took off and left the job unfinished. Daniel helped me out."

"That sounds like him." Chloe signed the credit card slip the woman pushed toward her, her mind racing. Had Daniel slept with this woman? Helping out was like Daniel; sleeping with other women wasn't. She felt as if she'd entered an alternate universe. "Did he say where he was going after he left here?"

"To the coast. He missed being near the water." She paused. "Have you come to take him home?"

Maybe it was the woman's receptive manner or maybe the fact that Daniel had known her, but something made Chloe say with a sad half smile, "I've come to let him go."

The woman gave her a long, assessing look. Then she took down a key from the board on the wall behind her. "I've put you in one of the rooms he finished. He did a good job." She paused. "He's a good man."

"He is, isn't he?" Chloe took the key and started for the door. "I'll be leaving first thing in the morning, so I might not see you."

"Wait."

Chloe turned, half expecting unwanted revelations.

The woman held out bath and hand towels. "So I don't have to disturb you later."

The unit was spacious compared to most motel rooms, with a separate bedroom and a combined kitchenette and sitting room. Chloe walked through all the rooms, running her hands over door frames and cabinets, noting how every timber was straight and true. She imagined Daniel working in here—his broad shoulders flexing as he hammered, the tiny grunt he gave when he picked up a heavy load, his habit of pushing a hand through his hair while he pondered a problem.

She was too tired to go out again and grateful for the supplies she'd brought from Adelaide and the means to cook a simple meal. She took her toasted sandwich out to the verandah and watched the trees fill with birds. The woman came out of the office and slowly made her way around the yard as she watered the geraniums that grew alongside the units. She had heavy breasts and a thick waist and she moved as if she were low on gas. Not a serious threat—unless Daniel was looking for someone as unlike Chloe as possible.

Chloe was dusting the crumbs off her hands when the woman approached her. She reached into the pocket of her shorts and withdrew a postcard. "This just came last week."

The picture was of a row of brightly colored beach huts, with the caption, Mornington bathing boxes. Chloe flipped it over and the sight of Daniel's familiar handwriting made her heart clench.

Good to wet my feet again. Thanks for everything. Daniel.

"Where's Mornington?" Chloe asked.

"Southeast of Melbourne on Port Phillip Bay." The woman poured a dribble of water over the dusty plants, then started to move away. "Tell him Ingrid said hello."

"I'll do that." Chloe tried to hand back the card.

"Keep it," Ingrid said as she met Chloe's eyes with her own. "He still loves you."

Chloe bit her lip. Part of her wanted to scream, *You*

don't know anything about Daniel and me. Part of her wanted to lay her head on Ingrid's bosom and cry— as perhaps Daniel had done. Instead she just nodded. "We'll see."

"Danno!" Glen called out as he walked through the house they were framing, the sound of his boot-steps hollow on the plywood underflooring. "Someone's lookin' for you."

Daniel lowered the cordless screwdriver and wiped a forearm across his sweaty brow. "Who?"

He knew no one in Mornington except for the guys he worked with. He might have a beer with them after work, but other than that he pretty much kept to himself.

"Some sheila," Glen said. "She's hot, mate, so if you don't want her stand back and give the rest of us a go."

"You think anything in a skirt is hot," Daniel joked. He just hoped she wasn't a government official who'd discovered he was working illegally. There was a housing boom on, and with carpenters in short supply contractors were happy to pay under the table for a good worker. But that didn't mean he wouldn't be fined or ordered to leave the country if he was caught. Daniel shoved the drill into his tool belt and walked through the skeleton of the house to where the front door would eventually be.

His heart stopped. Chloe, in a thin, lacy top and

a cotton skirt too light for the Melbourne winter, waited there. Her bright hair glowed against the dark green of a hedge and her bare legs were turned out in the characteristic dancer's pose. When she saw him her lips curved in a spontaneous smile, which she quickly dampened.

"Who is it?" Glen asked, at his shoulder.

"My wife." A surge of joy filled him, tempered by pain. More beautiful even than he'd remembered, she still seemed like a stranger to him.

"Bloody hell! You're a dark horse. What're you waiting for?" Glen said. "Go on, mate, get out of here."

Daniel glanced at his watch. Only ten minutes to knock off, anyway. "Thanks. See you tomorrow."

He strode over and took Chloe's arm to hustle her away from Glen's curious gaze. Her cool skin was covered with goose bumps and he resisted the urge to rub warmth into her. "What are you doing in that getup? You'll freeze."

"I thought Australia was warm everywhere," she said.

"Not in winter. What are you doing here, anyway?" They went across the road to a bus stop, to shelter from the cool breeze. Daniel searched her face for clues to her sudden appearance, but her expression was wary. She'd always worn her emotions in her eyes; now she was giving away nothing.

"You've been gone nearly six months." She pulled

away from his grip and wrapped her arms around herself. "We need to talk."

The phrase put dread in his stomach. He'd known all along that sooner or later he'd have to face Chloe and his responsibilities back home. But although he'd found a measure of peace within himself, he was still searching for some important answers. He wasn't ready to make decisions. For now life was bearable because it was uncomplicated, the way it had been twenty years ago before Chloe, before Brianna. Before love.

"My truck's over here." He jerked a thumb over his shoulder at the secondhand black van he'd just purchased.

"I'm driving a rental car," she said, nodding to a red Holden. "I'll follow you."

Daniel got into his truck and waited for her before pulling onto the road. He drove through residential streets to the esplanade, stopping in one of the small parking lots overlooking the bay. Chloe pulled in beside him and Daniel got into the passenger side of her car.

"How did you find me?" he asked.

Her gaze swept from the boats anchored in the water to the brightly colored bathing boxes lining the curving beach. "Ingrid says hello."

"Ah, I see." He was damned if he'd apologize for Ingrid. He studied Chloe's profile. She looked older in some indefinable way, though her skin was no more lined than it had been when he'd left Vancouver Island. "Did you like Coober Pedy?"

The sudden lilt of her laughter assaulted him with memories of a piercing sweetness. "How did *you* last eight weeks in a cave in a desert?"

He chuckled. "Maybe I was a bear in a previous life. There were times I felt like going into hibernation."

Their smiles faded as their eyes locked. He wanted to tell her how much he'd missed her; how he'd listened to her voice on his cell phone and had to force himself not to answer. He wanted to tell her that he loved her.

She reached for her purse, which was tucked on the floor of the back seat and pulled out an envelope.

"What's this?" He dangled it by a corner, as if it contained a letter bomb.

"Separation papers. I had Smitty draw them up for us. The terms are straightforward, but if there's anything you don't agree with we can talk about it. If they're fine, you can sign them and we can…" Her voice broke and she cleared her throat. "Move on. Later, we can divorce."

"Leaving you free to marry Evan," he said flatly.

She glanced at him. "I won't be marrying Evan. I told you, it's over between the two of us."

Daniel had been so sure that once Chloe'd gotten over the emotional upheaval of his departure she would run to Evan. For a moment he couldn't speak. Finally he cleared his throat. "You haven't seen him this trip?"

She shook her head. "Ironic, but there it is. I feel sorry for him, to tell you the truth."

"Don't waste your compassion," Daniel said brusquely. "He's selfish, deceitful and egotistical."

Chloe sighed heavily. "You're right."

With that acknowledgment, Daniel felt a massive weight lift from his chest. After all these years he could finally say what he thought, without Chloe defending the jerk.

Before he could go on, Chloe asked softly, "What was Ingrid to you?"

Daniel was quiet for a moment, remembering the interlude of mutual healing he'd experienced with Ingrid. Neither had expected anything from the other but a warm body to hold in the night. She had saved him from his self-destructive impulses and he'd been her bridge from loss and grief back to the world of feeling. He'd finished the work on her motel and as a parting gift she'd given him the runaway builder's tools. Then he'd gone on his way knowing neither had regrets even though they'd never see each other again.

"She was a drink of water when I was dying of thirst."

Chloe made a half smile. "Ingrid saved your life. What have *I* done for you? Or should I say, *to* you." Before he could reply, she laid a tentative hand on his knee. "I am truly sorry, Daniel. You deserved a faithful, loving wife. I let you down."

His throat closed and he couldn't speak, so he

simply shrugged. The envelope containing their separation papers lay next to her fingers. She seemed to notice at the same time and withdrew her hand.

Daniel reminded himself to breathe. "Have you seen Brianna?"

"Yes!" Chloe seemed relieved at the change of subject. "She's settled into her courses and college life. Oh—"

"What?"

"She asked Evan about her paternity."

Daniel's eyebrows rose. A pulse began to beat erratically in his temple. "Does he know something we don't?"

"Apparently he had DNA tests done when she was a baby and he didn't tell us. It must have been the time she choked and we took her to the hospital," Chloe said. "Anyway, it proved *you* are her biological father."

Daniel leaned back in his seat and stared straight ahead, letting the news sink in. He'd always believed Brianna's paternity didn't matter, so why did he feel this deep joy, this surge of triumph? He couldn't love her any more than he already did but...

Ah, that was it. Knowing she was his daughter severed the last tenuous connection of his family to Evan.

"I wonder why Brianna didn't tell me herself."

"She thought I should be the one."

"Well, I'm glad. I'll give her a call. I was planning on working my way back up north to Brisbane, but it's taken longer than I thought." He wiped his palms over his pants, suddenly aware of how dirty he was. "Where are you staying?"

"At a motel up the road. I just got in last night." Chloe paused. When she spoke again her voice had tightened. "What about you? Do you have another Ingrid?"

He shook his head. "There hasn't been anyone else and I'm not looking. Ingrid wasn't some kind of payback, you know. It just happened. I didn't feel like I was your husband anymore."

"You don't have to explain," she said quickly. "To tell you the truth, I don't want to know." She spread her hands, trying to explain. "It's not relevant."

Did that mean she no longer cared? Daniel gripped the envelope. He was damned if he'd allow their marriage to be signed away. "Listen, I'm going back to my motel room to clean up. Would you like to get together for dinner? There's a great seafood place down by the pier."

The wariness in her eyes receded and she smiled. "I'd like that very much. In the meantime, I'll go buy some warmer clothing."

Chloe found a department store and bought a pair of jeans and a couple of sweaters to tide her over until she returned home. Things weren't turning out the way she'd hoped. All during the long drive back to Adelaide and then across to Melbourne she'd fantasized that Daniel would tell her he loved her and toss the papers out the window. Instead, he'd taken them away to sign.

She was slowly making her way up Main Street when a gorgeous dress in a boutique window caught her eye. If she and Daniel were going to mark the occasion of their separation with a restaurant meal, she might as well exit the marriage looking her best.

Of course, that meant having her hair done, too.

And her nails.

And buying a new pair of shoes.

It wasn't over till it was over.

Three hours later, she was feeling less like a piece of tumbleweed that had blown in off the desert and more like a woman who might interest a man. When she opened the door of her motel unit to Daniel, she was glad she'd made an effort.

"Right on time." She ran her gaze over his tall figure, noting the changes she'd missed when she'd seen him in his work clothes. His muscular frame was leaner than when he'd left back in January and his face had a hint of the ascetic in the lean freshly shaven jaw and the far-seeing gaze. His clothes, good pants and a shirt she'd never seen before, were stylish. He was a very handsome man. She'd always known it, but now his attractiveness struck her anew. Just as she was about to lose him.

"You look great." His eyes drank her in with equal fascination. "Got the works, did you?"

Chloe blushed, pleased that he'd noticed and embarrassed at the same time. "Had to get that desert dust out of my pores," she said lightly. Then she reached for an envelope she'd left on the side table. "This is for you. It's a summary of your business accounts while you've been gone."

Daniel made a face. "Poor Rob. That's the only thing I felt bad about, leaving him with the accounts, when he wasn't used to it and had so much else to take care of."

"*I* did them," Chloe said. "And they all balance. You can check if you like." Enjoying the look of surprise on his face, she picked up her purse. "Shall we go?"

It was like a date, she thought as he held the car door open for her. She smiled up at him and his hand brushed her shoulder, sending a jolt through her.

The restaurant was built on stilts right over the water and had a deck that commanded sweeping views up and down the bay, with the lights of Melbourne twinkling in the distance. The sun had set on the far shore, but the sky still glowed red, shedding a ruddy glow across the water. Masthead lights winked on some of the boats bobbing nearby and fishermen at the end of the pier were silhouetted against the evening sky.

Daniel had reserved a table near the window. Chloe glanced around at the linen-clad tables and the original artwork depicting local seascapes. "This is lovely."

"The food is good, too. Or so I've heard."

The waiter brought the wine list and Chloe reached for it automatically. Daniel, eyebrows raised in mild admonishment, took it from her hands. He studied it a moment then handed it back to the waiter. "We'll have the 2003 Mintaro Chardonnay, thanks."

"You've become a wine buff?" she asked, not quite believing Daniel's new self-assurance.

"Don't look so surprised. I spent a month in the Barossa Valley helping build a winery," he explained. "Did a bit of tasting in my spare time, talking to vintners. You can't help but pick up a bit of knowledge."

"So what else have you been doing with yourself?" She was captivated by the idea of him living a whole other life than the one they'd shared. It made him mysterious and exciting in a way she hadn't thought of him being before.

The waiter came back with the wine and waited for Daniel's approval before pouring them both a glass and leaving the bottle in an ice bucket.

Daniel's blunt fingers wrapped around the stem of his wineglass. Although his hands were rough and calloused, his fingernails, as always, were clean. "After I left Brianna I just drove. I saw a lot of sights, though I can't say I remember much about them. Not until I stopped in Coober Pedy did I start to lose that numb feeling."

"And since then?"

"The winery, a few handyman jobs, anything I could get, where the employer was willing to look the other way when it came to paperwork." He grinned. "Did you see that giant koala on the side of the highway when you drove across from Adelaide? I repaired his ears after he was struck by lightning."

Chloe laughed out loud. "I loved that koala!"

"What about you?" he asked. "How're your classes going?"

"Really well," she said. "One of my pupils, Renee, has won a place with Ballet Victoria. She doesn't start till September, so she's teaching my classes for me while I'm down here."

"It's a shame you had to give up your soloist position years ago," Daniel said. "You were something special."

"How would you know?" she asked, her smile fading. "You never saw me dance."

"Sure I did. I just didn't let you know I was there."

"What?" she said, astounded and confused. "Why not?"

"I didn't exactly fit in with your fancy ballet friends, did I?" he said with a self-mocking grimace. "You would have had to introduce me around, hiding your embarrassment at having such a philistine for a husband."

"No!" Chloe began, then subsided. There was a grain of truth there. She sat back in her chair, staring at him as if she'd never seen him before. "I wish I'd known you saw me. I always thought you viewed my dancing as frivolous."

His gaze grew dreamy. "You were like a fairy princess, flitting around on your tippy toes. I wanted to take you home in my pocket and put you on the mantelpiece." Then his gaze drifted to her breasts. "Mind you, I also fantasized about storming the stage, pushing up your tutu and having hot, raunchy sex with you in front of the audience, to the roar of applause."

"Good grief, Daniel!" Chloe laughed even as her cheeks burned.

He shrugged. "I was a little conflicted."

Still grinning, she added, "You always did like to do it out in the open."

"I don't recall you complaining." His smile gentled and touched her heart with a wrenching tenderness. "We had some good times together, didn't we?"

"We sure did." The air thickened with unspoken yearning. Chloe felt her eyes blur and reached for her menu to hide behind. "What looks good?"

Daniel curled one finger over the top of her menu and pulled it down. "Do you really want me to sign that separation agreement?"

Heart pounding, unable to speak, she shook her head.

"I can't go back to the way we were," he said.

His honesty was searing. Her heart sank. "What is it you want?"

"To begin my life again."

She swallowed. "Without me?"

He shook his head and reached across the table to take both her hands in his. "We never had a courtship. You were this beautiful, unattainable creature I won by default. In some ways, I'd almost like to divorce, just so we could start completely fresh with no obligations on either side."

"That would be a waste of time and money," she pointed out.

"What have you done with my Chloe?" he asked with a smile. "Who's this practical lady sitting in her seat?"

Love burned in her heart at the fondly possessive, *my Chloe*. "I've had to learn how to do a lot of things I never did when you were at home," she said. "I even built a new bookcase."

"Good for you," he said admiringly.

"I guess we've both changed," she said sadly. "You've learned you can live without me."

"I don't exactly know all I can and can't do. I'm just finding out a lot of things. I left home because my heart was broken, but it's turned into an odyssey of self-discovery." He paused. "What do *you* want out of life?"

"Like you, I want to continue finding out who I am. Part of that is learning new skills, developing new interests." That didn't mean she wanted to part from him. But the time for pleading was past; she needed him to want her back. "Well, what do you propose we do about us?"

"I'm heading north in a few days. Why don't you come with me? We don't need to make any decisions. We'll meander up the coast and take whatever comes along."

Light-headed with relief, Chloe squeezed his hands. "That sounds good to me."

Daniel leaned over the table and French-kissed her right in front of the approaching waiter, as if they were teenagers instead of a middle-aged long-time married couple. Chloe swallowed her laughter and kissed him back. She had a feeling this trip would turn into the honeymoon they'd never had.

And with a bit of luck, sooner or later the road they traveled just might lead them home.

Epilogue

"Mom! Dad! I'm going down to the beach now." Ten-year-old Thanh ran out of the house with fins, mask and snorkel slung over his spindly arms. His bare feet thudded on the wooden decking as he raced past Chloe, who was carrying a tray of salmon steaks out to the barbecue. Thanh's best friend, a towheaded boy named Jason, waited on the lawn, similarly encumbered with snorkeling gear.

"Stay close to shore," Daniel cautioned, following Chloe with a platter of hamburgers. "And don't lose sight of each other. Not for a second."

"Don't be long," Chloe called. "The party's starting in half an hour and our guests will be arriving soon."

"We will. We won't. We…" Getting confused, Thanh shrugged and flashed his parents a sunny smile before disappearing down the path through the salal bushes, yelling, "Come on, Jase. Race you to the water."

Shaking her head, Chloe exchanged an indulgent smile with Daniel. A year after they'd returned from Australia they'd made a trip to Vietnam to adopt a six-month-old baby boy. Thanh was the son Daniel had always wanted and the second child Chloe had longed for. He was funny, cheerful and loving, a blessing on top of their already joyous lives.

"It's a perfect day for our anniversary party," Chloe said, setting the covered tray of salmon on the picnic table. She glanced up at a cloudless blue sky and breathed in air that was soft with the scent of apple blossoms. "When do I get to see your mysterious present?" she asked, nodding at a tarp-shrouded, waist-high object set into the lawn.

"Soon," he promised. Then he shook his head as if in disbelief. "Just think, we've been married thirty years. And I've turned fifty-one!"

"You don't look a day over forty-five." Chloe slipped her arms around his waist. It was true; he kept himself in good shape, and although his hair was now an attractive gray he looked years younger than his age. Their marriage had never been stronger and not a day went by that she didn't thank her lucky stars she had had the good sense to marry him. It still scared her, to think how close they'd come to breaking up.

"You're such a comfort to me in my old age," Daniel replied, adopting a doddery quaver. Then he switched back to his normal voice. "Just wait till you turn the big five-oh next year."

"Bring it on," Chloe said, smiling. "I've never felt healthier or happier in my life."

"You've certainly never been more beautiful," Daniel said, kissing her on the neck. "Or sexier. How much time do we have before everyone gets here?"

His broad hands spanned her waist as he effortlessly lifted her off her feet and started carrying her toward the hammock strung between the apple tree and a plum tree.

"Daniel, put me down!" Chloe said, laughing. "Remember what happened last time we got in the hammock together?"

"I most certainly do," he said with a wicked grin. "I've been looking forward to a repeat performance."

"You mean of the part where the hammock collapses with us in it?" She wriggled in his arms but that just made him hold her more tightly, which was actually pretty nice.

"I was thinking of the scene before that," he said.

"You mean—"

Daniel's mouth came down on hers, abruptly cutting off further discussion. Twining her arms around his neck, she gave herself up to the kiss. The sun beat down on her bare shoulders and his cotton shirt was hot beneath her palms. He let her slide down his body till she felt the grass between her bare toes. Then he whispered something in her ear that sent a wave of heat washing over her.

"Stop it!" she said, scandalized and thrilled. Ever since he'd realized that his fantasies about making love in odd places tickled her fancy, he'd given free rein to expressing them. She, in turn, had been inspired to come up with a few erotic scenarios of her own, which they took delight in acting out. It kept things interesting.

Daniel was just starting to lower her into the hammock when Brianna called through the open doors, "Is anybody home?"

"We're out here." Chloe struggled to her feet and quickly smoothed her hair back into place. "Goodness, what will Charlie think of us?"

"Maybe he'll reckon like mother, like daughter, and think he's hit the jackpot," Daniel suggested.

Chloe didn't have a chance to retort because Brianna and her Australian husband had come through the patio doors onto the deck.

"She's gained a little weight," Daniel murmured, surprised.

Chloe elbowed him. "Shh, don't you dare say anything."

True, Brianna looked as though she'd gained a couple of pounds, but she was prettier than ever. Charlie looked the same as Chloe remembered him— tall and lean, with chestnut-colored hair brushed back from a high forehead and dark green eyes that crackled with dry humor. Like Brianna, he was a marine biologist. They'd only met Charlie on a few occasions over the years and Chloe was always left wishing they had more time to get to know the easy-going Aussie who'd convinced Brianna—a determined singleton—to marry.

"Happy anniversary, Mom and Dad." Brianna crossed the lawn to hug them both. "I've got your present in my suitcase. I'll get it in a minute."

"You should have let me pick you up from the airport instead of hiring a rental car," Daniel said, taking Charlie's hand and clasping his shoulder in greeting.

"We needed a car, anyway." Charlie's eyebrows rose as he glanced at Brianna. "Do you want to tell them?"

"Tell us what?" Chloe glanced from Charlie to Brianna, who was flushed and smiling. "What's this about the rental car?"

"We need to drive around…to look for a house to buy." Brianna laughed, unable to contain her excitement. "We're moving back here! Charlie got a job at the Patricia Bay research institute."

Tears sprang to Chloe's eyes and she pulled Brianna back into a crushing hug. "Oh, my goodness. That's wonderful. What about you? Have you got a job, too?"

Brianna's smile widened. "I'm not looking right away. You see, I'm going to have a baby."

Chloe shrieked. "A baby! Daniel, we're going to be grandparents."

"I can't think of a better anniversary present." Daniel hugged Brianna and Charlie, too. "We'd better open the champagne."

"Mineral water for me," Brianna said.

"Charlie, want to give me a hand?" Daniel led the way inside, saying, "You and Brianna should think about buying land. I'd be happy to build you a house."

Chloe hugged Brianna again. "I'm so glad you're coming home. We've missed you so much."

"I've missed you, too." Brianna glanced around. "Where's Thanh? I brought him a shark jaw, like I promised."

"He's snorkeling with Jason. They should be back shortly," Chloe said. "Come and sit down. Tell me what you've been doing."

Brianna took a seat in a chair across from Chloe. "Do you remember Evan?"

Chloe's eyebrows rose. She rarely thought of Evan these days, but of course she hadn't forgotten him. "Why?"

"He was on TV the other week, talking about an international task force he's heading up aimed at eradicating malaria," Brianna said. "Apparently, he's married now. During his interview, he mentioned that he and his wife, who is also a doctor, would spend the next twelve months living and working in Africa."

So Evan was married. Chloe searched her heart for any lingering regret that she and Evan had never gotten together. She found none. But she was pleased, for Evan's sake, that he'd found someone who shared his passion. For all his faults he *had* dedicated his life to helping others.

"Good for him." Chloe heard footsteps and turned to see Daniel and Charlie coming back with drinks.

Daniel popped the cork and filled three crystal flutes with foaming champagne and Brianna's with mineral water. They raised their glasses in a series of toasts—to the baby, the move, Daniel's birthday and his and Chloe's anniversary.

Thanh and Jason came back through the bushes, wet and sandy, their snorkels and fins dangling from their hands. Thanh saw Brianna and came running. "Did you bring me a shark jaw?"

"I certainly did, squirt." With a sidelong wink at Daniel, she added, "I caught it myself."

"Holy cow!" Thanh turned to Daniel, aggrieved. "How come you never let *me* go shark hunting?"

Daniel laughed. "I'd hope you'd have more sense."

Brianna took Thanh and Jason off to find the shark jaw and Charlie said he'd get the suitcases out of the car.

Chloe gazed after them, her eyes blurring with happy tears. "Life just keeps getting better and better." She blinked and dragged in a breath. "Gosh, I'm feeling emotional today."

Daniel cupped her chin and kissed away the

moisture. "Long ago you said to me, 'Ingrid saved your life. What have *I* done for you?'"

"I remember," Chloe murmured. "You'd given me so much, your love had always been so true and steadfast, I wished I could do the same for you."

"You brought me to life," Daniel said. "Before I met you I was just a hammer jockey, working and waiting—for what, I didn't know. From the moment I saw you in that Laundromat, I knew *you* were my future. Everything I've accomplished has been at least partly because of you or for you. Without you, my life wouldn't be the same."

Chloe smiled, feeling a lump in her throat. "When I met you I felt like *my* life was over, that the world as I knew it had ended. Little did I know you would open the door to a better world. It took me a long time to realize that, but thank goodness I did."

"Here's to another thirty years." Daniel touched his glass to hers with a soft clink. "Together, forever."

Chloe sipped the sparkling wine, tiny bubbles fizzing and popping in front of her eyes as she gazed over the rim at her beloved husband.

Daniel set their glasses aside. "Come, it's time to show you my present."

He led her to the shrouded object and pulled off the black tarp. The afternoon sun illuminated a marble sundial with a bronze blade to mark the hours. "Read the inscription."

Chloe traced the engraved words with a finger.

"'Grow old with me, the best is yet to be.'" She turned to him, her eyes misting. "Oh, Daniel."

Dimly, Chloe heard the doorbell, followed by the sound of voices and laughter spilling through their home. She drew back gently to meet Daniel's gaze in a last intimate look, then hand in hand they went to greet their guests. It was party time and they had so much to celebrate.

★ ★ ★ ★ ★

THE ROYAL HOUSE OF NIROLI
Always passionate, always proud

The richest royal family in the world—united by
blood and passion, torn apart by deceit and desire

Nestled in the azure blue of the Mediterranean Sea, the
majestic island of Niroli has prospered for centuries.
The Fierezza men have worn the crown with passion
and pride since ancient times. But now, as the king's
health declines, and his two sons have been tragically
killed, the crown is in jeopardy.

The clock is ticking—a new heir must be found
before the king is forced to abdicate. By royal decree the
internationally scattered members of the Fierezza family
are summoned to claim their destiny. But any person
who takes the throne must do so according to The Rules
of the Royal House of Niroli. Soon secrets and rivalries
emerge as the descendents of this ancient royal line
vie for position and power. Only a true Fierezza can
become ruler—a person dedicated to their country, their
people…and their eternal love!

Each month starting in July 2007,
Harlequin Presents is delighted to bring you
an exciting installment from
THE ROYAL HOUSE OF NIROLI,
in which you can follow the epic search
for the true Nirolian king.
Eight heirs, eight romances, eight fantastic stories!

Here's your chance to enjoy a sneak preview of the
first book delivered to you by royal decree…

FIVE minutes later she was standing immobile in front of the study's window, her original purpose of coming in forgotten, as she stared in shocked horror at the envelope she was holding. Waves of heat followed by icy chill surged through her body. She could hardly see the address now through her blurred vision, but the crest on its left-hand front corner stood out, its *royal* crest, followed by the address: *HRH Prince Marco of Niroli*...

She didn't hear Marco's key in the apartment door, she didn't even hear him calling out her name. Her shock was so great that nothing could penetrate it. It encased her in a kind of bubble, which only concentrated the torment of what she was suffering and branded it on her brain so that it could never be forgotten. It was only finally pierced by the sudden opening of the study door as Marco walked in.

"Welcome home, *Your Highness*. I suppose I ought to curtsy." She waited, praying that he would laugh and tell her that she had got it all wrong, that the envelope she was holding, addressing him as Prince Marco of Niroli, was some silly mistake. But like a tiny candle flame shivering vulnerably in the dark, her hope trembled fearfully. And then the look in Marco's eyes extinguished it as cruelly as a hand placed callously over a dying person's face to stem their last breath.

"Give that to me," he demanded, taking the envelope from her.

"It's too late, Marco," Emily told him brokenly. "I know the truth now...." She dug her teeth in her lower lip to try to force back her own pain.

"You had no right to go through my desk," Marco shot back at her furiously, full of loathing at being caught off-guard and forced into a position in which he was in the wrong, making him determined to find something he could accuse Emily of. "I trusted you...."

Emily could hardly believe what she was hearing. "No, you didn't trust me, Marco, and you didn't trust me because you knew that I couldn't trust you. And you knew that because you're a liar, and liars don't trust people because they know that they themselves cannot be trusted." She not only felt sick, she also felt as though she could hardly breathe. "You are Prince Marco of Niroli.... How could you not tell me who you are and still live with me as intimately as we have lived together?" she demanded brokenly.

"Stop being so ridiculously dramatic," Marco

demanded fiercely. "You are making too much of the situation."

"*Too much?*" Emily almost screamed the words at him. "When were you going to tell me, Marco? Perhaps you just planned to walk away without telling me anything? After all, what do my feelings matter to you?"

"Of course they matter." Marco stopped her sharply. "And it was in part to protect them, and you, that I decided not to inform you when my grandfather first announced that he intended to step down from the throne and hand it on to me."

"To protect me?" Emily nearly choked on her fury. "Hand on the throne? No wonder you told me when you first took me to bed that all you wanted was sex. You *knew* that was the only kind of relationship there could ever be between us! You *knew* that one day you would be Niroli's king. No doubt you are expected to marry a princess. Is she picked out for you already, your *royal* bride?"

★ ★ ★ ★ ★

Look for
**THE FUTURE KING'S
PREGNANT MISTRESS**
*by Penny Jordan in July 2007,
from Harlequin Presents,
available wherever books are sold.*

Silhouette®

Romantic
SUSPENSE

**Sparked by Danger,
Fueled by Passion.**

Mission: Impassioned

A brand-new miniseries begins with

My Spy

By *USA TODAY* bestselling author

Marie Ferrarella

She had to trust him with her life....
It was the most daring mission of Joshua Lazlo's
career: rescuing the prime minister of England's
daughter from a gang of cold-blooded kidnappers.
But nothing prepared the shadowy secret agent
for a fiery woman whose touch ignited something
far more dangerous.

My Spy

#1472

Available July 2007 wherever you buy books!

REQUEST YOUR FREE BOOKS!

2 FREE NOVELS PLUS 2 FREE GIFTS!

 HARLEQUIN®

E V E R L A S T I N G   L O V E ™

Every great love has a story to tell™

YES! Please send me 2 FREE Harlequin® Everlasting Love™ novels and my 2 FREE gifts. After receiving them, if I don't wish to receive any more books, I can return the shipping statement marked "cancel." If I don't cancel, I will receive 4 brand-new novels every other month and be billed just $4.47 per book in the U.S. or $4.99 per book in Canada, plus 25¢ shipping and handling per book and applicable taxes, if any*. That's a savings of about 15% off the cover price! I understand that accepting the 2 free books and gifts places me under no obligation to buy anything. I can always return a shipment and cancel at any time. Even if I never buy another book from Harlequin, the two free books and gifts are mine to keep forever.

153 HDN ELX4 353 HDN ELYG

Name	(PLEASE PRINT)	
Address		Apt.
City	State/Prov.	Zip/Postal Code

Signature (if under 18, a parent or guardian must sign)

Mail to the **Harlequin Reader Service**®:
IN U.S.A.: P.O. Box 1867, Buffalo, NY 14240-1867
IN CANADA: P.O. Box 609, Fort Erie, Ontario L2A 5X3

Not valid to current Harlequin Everlasting Love subscribers.

Want to try two free books from another line?
Call 1-800-873-8635 or visit www.morefreebooks.com.

* Terms and prices subject to change without notice. NY residents add applicable sales tax. Canadian residents will be charged applicable provincial taxes and GST. This offer is limited to one order per household. All orders subject to approval. Credit or debit balances in a customer's account(s) may be offset by any other outstanding balance owed by or to the customer. Please allow 4 to 6 weeks for delivery.

Your Privacy: Harlequin is committed to protecting your privacy. Our Privacy Policy is available online at www.eHarlequin.com or upon request from the Reader Service. From time to time we make our lists of customers available to reputable firms who may have a product or service of interest to you. If you would prefer we not share your name and address, please check here. ☐

HEL07

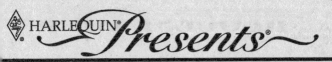

Always passionate, always proud.

**The richest royal family in the world—
a family united by blood and passion,
torn apart by deceit and desire.**

Step into the glamorous, enticing world of the
Nirolian Royal Family. As the king ails he must find an
heir...each month an exciting new installment follows
the epic search for the true Nirolian king. Eight heirs,
eight romances, eight fantastic stories!

It's time for playboy prince Marco Fierezza to
claim his rightful place...on the throne of Niroli!
Emily loves Marco, but she has no idea he's a royal
prince! What will this king-in-waiting do when he
discovers his mistress is pregnant?

THE FUTURE KING'S
PREGNANT MISTRESS

by Penny Jordan

(#2643)

On sale July 2007.

www.eHarlequin.com

HP12643

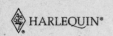

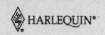

EVERLASTING LOVE™

Every great love has a story to tell™

COMING NEXT MONTH

#11. *The Letter* by Elizabeth Blackwell

Cassie has always thought her grandparents had the perfect marriage. Henry and Lydia were high-school sweethearts, and their relationship is the foundation on which Cassie relies. But when she finds an old, impassioned love letter hidden with Lydia's quilting supplies, Cassie is forced to reconsider everything she thought she knew. The letter is signed "F.B."—not her grandfather's initials. Who is the mysterious writer and what does this mean for Cassie's family?

An engaging and beautifully written story from a debut author.

#12. *Snapshots* by Pamela Browning

Snapshots—moments of our lives captured for all time, a way to hold on to the past. For Rick McCullough and Trista Barrineau, who are thrown together one weekend at Sweetwater Cottage in the South Carolina Low Country, snapshots of a past life could trigger a love long buried. A love that began when they were teenagers—before Rick married Martine, Trista's twin....

An intriguing new book from a longtime popular author.

www.eHarlequin.com

HECNM0607